"I really appreciate what you're doing. I know I've turned your life, and whatever plans you had for your time in Hartley, upside down."

"You've helped me, too," he said.

She looked at him in surprise. "How? By helping you test your truck's braking system?"

He laughed, then shook his head. "I've had a tough time of it lately. Coping with all the details surrounding a loved one's death can be overwhelming. You've been a welcome, and beautiful, distraction."

As Lori looked into his dark eyes her heart began beating overtime. For those precious seconds, time stood still. She was aware of the warmth of his body and the spark of desire in his steady gaze.

"You're a mass of contradictions in one lovely package, Lori Baker," he whispered.

AIMÉE THURLO

POWER OF THE RAVEN

TORONTO NEW YORK LONDON
AMSTERDAM PARIS SYDNEY HAMBURG
STOCKHOLM ATHENS TOKYO MILAN MADRID
PRAGUE WARSAW BUDAPEST AUCKLAND

To Marilyn, who always has a smile for everyone.

Recycling programs
for this product may
not exist in your area.

ISBN-13: 978-0-373-74654-5

POWER OF THE RAVEN

Copyright © 2012 by Aimée and David Thurlo

ABOUT THE AUTHOR

Aimée Thurlo is a nationally known bestselling author. She's the winner of a Career Achievement Award from *RT Book Reviews*, a New Mexico Book Award in contemporary fiction and a Willa Cather Award in the same category. Her novels have been published in twenty countries worldwide.

She also cowrites the bestselling Ella Clah mainstream mystery series praised in the *New York Times* Book Review.

Aimée was born in Havana, Cuba, and lives with her husband of thirty-nine years in Corrales, New Mexico. Her husband, David, was raised on the Navajo Indian Reservation.

Books by Aimée Thurlo

HARLEQUIN INTRIGUE

Don't miss any of our special offers. Write to us at the following address for information on our newest releases.

Harlequin Reader Service
U.S.: 3010 Walden Ave., P.O. Box 1325, Buffalo, NY 14269
Canadian: P.O. Box 609, Fort Erie, Ont. L2A 5X3

CAST OF CHARACTERS

Gene Redhouse—His ranch and his mystical bond with animals ordered his life until a chance encounter with a woman on the run pushed him into a web of danger.

Lori Baker—Her stalker was relentless. She wanted her old life back, but with danger always just a half step away, there was no way out and no escape from her tormentor.

Duane Hays—The annoying wrangler had offended nearly every man and woman in the county, and he couldn't keep a job for more than a week. Word was, he'd do anything for money, and now he was in trouble again.

Daniel Hawk—He and Gene had stood back-to-back since their teens, and found safety and family with Hosteen Silver, the medicine man who'd taken them in. Now Dan was prepared to break every rule in the book for his foster brother.

Steve Farmer—The man worked beside Lori at the Motor Vehicle Department, but recently he seemed to have way too many problems with computers and passwords. Was he a con man, or the one being conned?

Bud Harrington—Bud was a jewelry designer and a sleeze ball, and Lori had not only rejected his advances, she'd reported him to the police. Now the authorities were running shorthanded and the time was ripe for payback.

Paul Grayhorse—He was a former U.S. Marshal and Gene's brother in every way that counted. If Gene and his woman needed his help, he'd be there for both of them, regardless of the cost.

Chapter One

There was nothing like death to make you appreciate life. His foster father, *Hosteen* Silver, hadn't been gone long, just a little over two months now, but his unexpected passing had reminded Gene Redhouse of just how unpredictable life really was.

Lifting the large bag of sweet feed his horses loved from the back of the truck, he glanced over at Grit. The horse, his foster father's favorite mount, was prancing around the corral, tossing his head and snorting. He was beautiful, with a graceful arched neck and a strong muscular body. A black-and-white pinto, Grit had a black head with a white blaze down his muzzle. The rest of him, legs included, was white except for the rounded black spots over his body.

"Maybe *Hosteen* Silver mixed up some of the letters he left for the six of us and I got yours by mistake. That's the only way things make sense, if you stop to think about it. Otherwise, why pick *me* to become friends with Grit?" Paul Grayhorse said, shaking his head. "You can communicate with animals in a way that's nothing short of amazing. If anyone can befriend that surly creature, it's you."

Gene glanced at his foster brother, who stood well back looking at the horse. Paul was tall and muscular, but the former U.S. Marshal was still stiff from the bullet that had sliced through his shoulder a few months back while on assignment protecting a federal judge.

"Be grateful he didn't ask you to climb up the cliff face to Winter Hawk's nest, like Daniel and I had to do," Gene said.

Paul nodded slowly. "Yeah." After a moment of silence, he continued, "When I first came out to the Rez with him, I thought he'd want us to call him by his first name, like the Anglo fosters did, but he explained that Navajos don't do that. Names have power and weren't to be used lightly. He said we should call him *Hosteen* Silver. I had no idea what that meant, and I think that surprised him. That's when he explained to me that *Hosteen* meant 'mister,' and Silver was the nickname others gave him because of his white hair. He also told me I could call him 'uncle,' if I preferred, since it also showed proper respect."

Gene smiled. "It was the same for Dan and me. To his face, we always called him 'uncle,' but now that he's gone, he remains *Hosteen* Silver to us."

"Hey, now that we're talking about him," Paul said, "do you have any more ideas why he left that

Changing-Bear-Maiden story for us in his safe-deposit box?"

"Not yet, but he did everything for a reason, like with those letters. I guess it's just another puzzle we'll have to figure out over time," Gene said.

Paul shrugged, flinching slightly with the gesture.

Although Paul had insisted on helping him unload the truck, Gene had taken the heavier sacks of feed and grain himself. "If I were you, I'd put off working with Grit awhile longer," Gene said. "You're still favoring your shoulder and there was no deadline on what *Hosteen* Silver asked you to do. Why not put it off until you're a hundred percent again?"

Paul shook his head. "Time meant little to *Hosteen* Silver, but I want to put this behind me."

"You'll have to rethink your tactics, then. You can't force a horse to do anything—they outweigh you, and they're stronger. You'll have to persuade and outthink him. I'd advise you to befriend Grit first with some apples or carrots. Get him to come to you. If you rush it, it'll be rodeo time and you'll get thrown. Count on it."

"Don't worry, I'll make it work. I'll start by lunging him and making sure he's tired." As Paul took the halter and lunge line, Grit, who'd been watching him, spun, bucked and started trotting around the corral. Finally, he ran to the far end of the corral, stopped and stared at them, ears pinned back.

"He's not in a good mood. If you try to corner

him now, he might just run over you," Gene said. "Back off for a while."

"Who are you kidding? That horse is *never* in a good mood," Paul said. "I remember when *Hosteen* Silver first brought that foul-tempered beast home. He asked me to exercise him, but every time I tried to ride him, I ended up facedown in the dirt. I was the one who named him Grit because that's what ended up in my mouth each time I was tossed."

"No big deal. The ground was there to catch you," Gene said, trying not to laugh.

Paul leaned against the fence rails and shot his brother a dirty look. "Eventually, you ended up with the job of riding him. *Hosteen* Silver knew that, one way or another, I'd always end up on the ground."

"That wasn't exactly a big secret, bro. You never showed Grit enough respect."

"It's a *horse*. You want me to bow?"

"As you said, Grit's a horse, not your Jeep," Gene said.

"Give me a Jeep any day of the week. Something goes wrong, you tune it up. It doesn't toss you flat on your butt just 'cause it's in a bad mood."

"Hang out and do nothing for a while. Let him watch you," Gene said. "I'm going to finish unloading."

Gene went to the tailgate, then climbed up into the bed of his truck. Just a few more mineral blocks to put away, then he'd start topping off the water troughs. Work at Two Springs Ranch never ended, but he loved it here. This was his world, a place that fit him perfectly.

Eventually, he intended to start looking around for a wife who enjoyed ranch life as much as he did, but love wasn't nearly as important to him as finding a compatible mate.

His brother's shouts broke through his thoughts.

"Get back!" Paul yelled.

Gene cursed and rushed out of the barn. Paul was trapped against the rails at the far corner of the corral. Grit had him blocked off completely, and was snorting and reaching out with his mouth, making repeated bite threats.

"Stop yelling," Gene said, slipping through the gate. "I thought you were going to wait."

"The fool thing played me! He looked like he'd calmed down, so I came over holding the halter. He let me get close, but when I tried to slip it over his head, he went nuts," Paul said, trying to sidestep past the horse. Grit shifted, blocking his way.

As Gene came up he sang a soft *Hozonji,* a good luck song *Hosteen* Silver had taught him. With each note, the animal visibly relaxed and soon Gene was able to reach out and grasp Grit by the mane.

"Back up," he said, clicking his tongue and tapping Grit on the chest. "Come on now, *back up!*"

The horse did as he was told, and Paul, seeing his chance, ducked out through the wooden rails of the corral. Once outside and in the clear, he waited for Gene to join him.

"If you say one word about patience, I'm going to deck you," Paul growled.

"Something set him off like that. You gonna tell me what really happened?"

Paul gave him a slow, sheepish grin. "My cell phone went off with that new Native American tribal drum ring tone."

"That's going to cost you big-time, bro," Gene said, shaking his head. "He won't forget it. You lost ground today."

"Yeah, I know." Paul expelled his breath through his teeth. "Grit's worse than ever, at least with me. These days he won't even let me get close."

"I think, in his own way, he misses *Hosteen* Silver. If it makes you feel any better, when he first came here, Grit had *me* running in circles—" Gene abruptly stopped speaking.

"What?"

"In the letter *Hosteen* Silver left for Dan and me, there was a special message at the bottom intended for me only. He said I'd see my future evolve from endless circles in the sand, and as the unlikely happened, the lost one would show me the way."

"Any idea what that means?"

"None, but maybe Grit will play a part," Gene said.

As they stepped out of the corral, a gentle breeze swept by, cooling Gene's sweat-soaked chest. "Wind's a messenger. Something's coming, a change maybe."

"Good or bad?" Paul asked.

"Things are good right now, so that narrows the options." Placing his hand over the medicine pouch on his belt, Gene looked at the storm clouds overhead and heard their ominous rumbling. "Time to start watching our backs."

Chapter Two

It was early evening in the town of Hartley and, after having supper at a local bar and grill, Gene was back on the road, looking forward to calling it a day. As executor of *Hosteen*'s trust, he'd agreed to take care of the paperwork that needed to be filed.

What he'd never realized until recently was just how time-consuming that would be. Although *Hosteen* had lived a simple life and had few possessions, the red tape had proved endless. Today he'd spent hours at the Department of Motor Vehicles transferring the title of *Hosteen*'s truck over to the Anglo who'd purchased it.

Knowing that Navajos, particularly Traditionalists and New Traditionalists, would want nothing to do with the possessions of the dead, he'd placed the ad in the Hartley paper, a town outside reservation borders. Though the truck was old, it was in remarkable shape, so it hadn't taken long to find a buyer after the first test drive.

Gene felt the weight of one less detail lift from his shoulders. Although they all missed their foster father, the heavy mantle of responsibility he'd accepted had prevented him from moving forward more than the others.

Yet he knew change was coming. He could feel it, like a stirring in his blood. He glanced down at the medicine pouch fastened onto his belt, then back to the road.

As Gene slowed to take a corner, a woman suddenly darted out into the street. Gene slammed on the brakes hard, skidding and burning rubber.

Cursing loudly, he came to a full stop. At least he'd managed to avoid hitting her. His heart was still racing when she ran up to the passenger door and opened it.

Thinking carjacking, Gene automatically reached for the rifle on the rack behind him. An instant later, he recognized the woman's face. He'd dealt with the clerk just a few hours ago at the motor vehicle department.

"Please, my name's Lori and I need your help. I stopped at Ofelia's Corner Diner to pick up some dinner, and when I came out I spotted a guy following me. Can you circle the block, then drop me off by my car? It isn't far."

"Jump in. Did you call the cops?"

"Several times, including earlier today when I noticed him following me to work," she said, climbing in and placing her big purse on the floor between her feet. "It took forever for an officer to respond this morning because of the current work slowdown—the blue flu. I stayed in my car like I was told, but by the time the officer got there, the guy had taken off. I think he figured I'd called for help and didn't want to get caught. Once he sees me drive off with you, he'll probably make himself real scarce again."

She shut the door and fastened the shoulder belt automatically. "My car's just down the block, so it'll only take a few minutes of your time."

"What's he look like? Can you still see him?" Gene checked the sidewalk up and down the street, using the side mirror.

She looked out the window. "He must have ducked out of sight. He was wearing a black jacket with a hood, sunglasses and a ball cap, same as this morning. He's close to six feet, average build, not overweight or skinny."

Gene studied her, taking in the soft hazel eyes and shoulder-length honey-brown hair, a subtle shade that would have been hard to get from a bottle. Her forest-green pullover sweater accentuated her beautiful breasts and hourglass figure.

No man with breath left in his lungs would ever forget meeting her. After dealing with her at the DMV, he'd expected her to haunt his dreams for some time. Now, here she was.

As the light changed to green, the vehicle behind him honked.

Moving forward again, Gene smiled. "Where to?" he asked. If things went sour, he still had his rifle and he could defend himself better than anyone he knew, including his brothers in law enforcement.

She pointed ahead. "It's not far. Just beyond that cottonwood. Once we're there, would you mind sticking around long enough for me to get in my car and drive off?"

"No problem."

She shifted in her seat and looked directly at him. "You look very familiar to me." She smiled slowly. "We met at the DMV earlier today, right?" Woven through her tentative smile was also a spark of interest.

He noted it, pleased. Gorgeous women like Lori didn't cross his path often, and after weeks of dealing with paperwork, a little excitement would do him a world of good.

"Yeah, I was there and you helped me with a title transfer," he said. He glanced in his rearview mirror but no one suspicious was following. "Do you happen to know the guy stalking you?" He'd been around his brothers in law enforcement long enough to have heard the stories. Old boyfriends and ex-husbands could turn a woman's life upside down.

"I can't be completely sure because I haven't been able to get a clear look at his face, but I suspect it's Bud Harrington, a man who keeps coming to my window at work. He wants to go out with me and won't take no for an answer."

"Have you told all that to the police?"

"Yeah, and to my boss, too." Lori pointed to an old cream-colored sedan up ahead. "That's my car. Thanks for helping me out, though I guess I didn't really give you much of a choice, did I?" She sent him an apologetic smile as he pulled to the curb and parked.

"You were smart to look for help when you did instead of trying to deal with the guy on your own." Though he liked fighting his own battles, the same rules didn't apply in this woman's case. Stalkers could become violent and she didn't have the right build to fight a man. She was about five foot two and all rounded corners and softness.

"Thanks for the ride." She looked around again as she opened the door, then froze. "He's there! Can you see him?"

"The guy in the black hooded windbreaker?"

"That's him, but without the ball cap this time. That hoodie covers part of his face, so I still can't tell for sure if it's Bud."

"Lock the door and wait here. Let me go talk to him."

As a former foster kid, he'd seen all the tough guys who liked to throw their weight around, the bullies who only picked on those who couldn't fight back and the ones who thought the world owed them. Street hoods came in all shapes and sizes, but they had one thing in common. They needed to vent their pent-up rage on someone and weren't interested in a fair fight.

Gene's walk was slow and steady, his gaze never leaving the man standing by the car. Though he still couldn't make out his face, Gene could see the name of the Hartley's high school team—the Scorpions—on his windbreaker.

Gene was within thirty yards of him when the man suddenly pivoted and took off at an all-out run. Gene chased him down the block, but the guy suddenly cut left, racing out into the street just as the light changed. Tires screeched, horns honked, but the runner made it across.

Gene tried to follow, but as he stepped out, a city bus turned the corner and blared its horn, forcing him to jump back. The bus pulled up to the curb right in front of him.

By the time Gene ran the length of the bus to the rear end, cars were racing by in both directions and the guy had vanished.

Gene cursed, but there was nothing more he could do now. This would have to remain a police problem. As he returned to his truck he saw Lori sitting there, looking around, searching for him.

She climbed out to greet him. "Are you okay?" she asked, handing him the key. "The second I saw him run off and you going after him, I called the police. I told them it was an emergency."

"Call them back. There's no hope of catching the guy now and they're stretched pretty tight. We may be taking them away from a real life-or-death situation, like a traffic accident."

She nodded and dialed quickly. After a second, she looked back at him. "As soon as I told them that there was no emergency, they put me on hold," she said with a grim smile. "It's all part of that slow-down. Negotiations between the city and the police department reached an impasse a week ago and neither side is giving an inch. Personally I side with the cops. They aren't getting paid enough, and if they end up having their benefits cut, too..." She shrugged and held her palms up. "Doesn't make much sense to stay in a job where you have to risk your life every day but still have to choose between paying the rent or your health insurance."

"True, but their situation sure doesn't help *you* much right now."

Someone finally answered the call, and Lori listened to the woman officer at the other end. "I'm sure this wasn't an attempt to steal my car," Lori told her. "I've got a sedan that's older than dirt. No one in their right mind would want it. And a purse snatching doesn't seem right, either. I do have my laptop inside, but you can't see it. If you check your records, I reported seeing a man following me this morning. Heck, I even blogged about it on my web-page during a coffee break."

A few seconds later, Lori hung up and focused on Gene. "In all the craziness, I don't think I introduced myself to you properly. You know my first name, but my last name's Baker," she said, extending her hand. "And you're Gene..."

He smiled. So she'd remembered his first name. This was turning out to be a good day, after all. "Gene Redhouse," he answered. Like most Navajos, he generally disliked touching strangers, even in a handshake, but he'd adapted to the Anglo custom. As he shook her hand, it surprised him how soft and small it felt in his.

For the first time since they'd met she gave him a full smile. Her whole face lit up and the effect took his breath away. She was heart-stopping gorgeous.

"Did the police say what they wanted you to do next?" he asked.

"They asked me to write down the details of what happened as soon as possible. Since no officer will be available for at least two hours, they want to make sure I don't forget anything. They'll also want to talk to you."

"Just to make sure I understand you, you gave the police the name of the man you think is stalking you?" he asked, verifying it. He remembered his brothers complaining about victims who protected their tormentors.

"Oh, sure, but Bud's a real creep. When I first filed harassment charges, he told the investigating officer that I'd come on to him and he even accused *me* of stalking *him*."

"So then it became your word against his?"

"Exactly," she said, and expelled her breath in a whoosh. "Reporting him not only got me nowhere, it brought my credibility into question."

"I don't think the police necessarily doubt your word," Gene said, "but their job requires them to rely solely on evidence. 'He said, she said' cases take a while to sort out."

"Maybe so, but it still stung. I wanted to force this guy to back off, but all I really did was create new problems for myself. Now, because he can't bother me at work without looking like a liar, I guess he's decided to follow me before and after hours. What scares me is that I'm not sure how far he's prepared to take this."

"How did you happen to spot him tonight? Were you looking for him?"

"I was on my guard, mostly because I'd had to park a little farther from the restaurant than I'd intended. After dinner I was walking back to my car and caught a glimpse of someone following me. I thought it was Bud, so I called out and told him to get lost. That didn't work, so I got scared. I ran out into the street to flag someone down."

"Which turned out to be me. But what made you think you weren't about to trade one problem for another?"

"Two sickos in a row? Not likely. As it was, I had no reason to think of you as a threat, but I knew the guy following me was trouble."

Gene didn't believe in coincidences. The universe had a pattern, and within that was order. Remembering *Hosteen*'s prediction, he suddenly wondered if Lori was somehow connected.

Hosteen Silver had mentioned circles, and Gene had been rounding a curve when she'd stepped out in front of his truck. Then again, *Hosteen* Silver had also written about a lost one who would show him the way, and neither Lori nor he had been lost. Maybe he was trying too hard to make sense of his foster father's prophecy.

Lori looked around slowly, then, as if making up her mind, met his gaze. "I'm not going to stay out here at this time of night, not with Bud wanting to make trouble for me. If the police want to question me, they can come to my home," she said. "They'll want to talk to you, too, so how about following me there? I could fix you something to eat, or if you've already eaten, we can have something to drink and snacks. It'll be my way of saying thanks. Then, after we talk to the police, you'll be free to be on your way," she said, and gave him one of her extraordinary smiles. "Or maybe you have a family to get home to...." she said, and looked down at his left hand, probably checking for signs of a wedding ring.

He smiled. She was totally irresistible. He had no particular plans tonight besides watching the basketball game on that monstrous set of Preston's. Staying at his brother's, who was currently out of town, had its perks.

"I'm not married and a drink and snacks sounds great," he said, accepting.

"Then follow me over to my place. I'll lead the way."

Her words sent a sudden chill up his spine. He wondered if this was the beginning of the change his foster father had predicted.

He walked with her to her car, then watched her fasten her seat belt, his gaze drifting over the graceful curve of her breasts. She probably had more than one secret admirer—not to mention her pick of men willing to keep her safe.

"I don't usually bring strangers home, but I think we both need to get out of the open."

"Yeah, good idea."

Moments later, he was in his truck following her to the main thoroughfare, then into an old residential neighborhood across town. Houses were crowded together here, too much so for his tastes. He liked lots of open space and clear views of the sky.

As she pulled into the driveway of a small house halfway down a narrow street, he noticed that she wasn't much for gardening. The outside was decorated with colored gravel and a few drought-resistant Southwest plants.

All things considered, he figured that whatever change was coming into his life wouldn't be likely to include Lori Baker. From what he'd seen of her so far, she was a town girl. The things that made her happy—like the high heels she wore and living in this crowded urban neighborhood—didn't fit in with the lifestyle of a hardworking rancher.

Still there was no harm in a quick drink. He was a single man with time on his hands, and a gorgeous woman had offered him a drink at her house. He would have been crazy to say no. He'd spend some time with her, no complications, no strings. It didn't get better than that.

He was just stepping down from his pickup when a hard gust of wind came right out of nowhere. It caught the door like a sail, forcing him to hold on to it to keep from springing the hinges.

Gene tucked in his chin and shut the door. As the gust swirled around him, peppering his face with fine dust, he thought he heard Wind's whispered warning—the danger had not yet passed.

Chapter Three

Gene went to meet Lori where she stood in front of
her closed garage door. "We weren't followed here.
I'm good at spotting things like that," he said, seeing
her looking around, a frown on her face.

"Okay, then. Let me put my car inside the garage,
then we can both go into the house and out of this
wind." She unlocked the single car garage's door
handle, gave it a twist, but nothing happened. "I got
a door installed that I could pull open, but I think
the springs are weak."

Gene stepped over and pulled it up for her.

"Thanks," she said.

Moments later her car was safely inside and the
door closed and locked. Gene followed her through
a side door.

He stepped inside what appeared to be a pantry,
then into the kitchen.

"My house is a work in progress. This room's already finished, so we can sit here without tripping
over paintbrushes and cans."

Gene followed her into the dining alcove that faced the front. "How long have you lived here?"

"I was born and raised in the Four Corners, but in this house, only about five months. I wanted to own, not rent, and I got a really good deal on this place. The important things like the heating and cooling and the plumbing all work fine, so I figured I'd add all the finishing touches as time and money allowed."

Lori waved him to a chair by the table, but he shook his head. "Let's find a place in the living room so I can have a better view of the front yard and street. I'd like to keep a lookout for a while longer."

"You think he'll come here?" she asked, her voice rising slightly.

"Even assuming he knows where you live, he probably wouldn't push it right now. This guy has no way of knowing what the police will do next, like maybe set up a neighborhood patrol. Still, it doesn't hurt to be careful."

"Maybe I should turn on more lights," she said, leading the way into the living room.

"Not necessary. The one in the kitchen is enough. Any more, and it'll be harder to see outside because of the glare on the windows," Gene said, walking past the ladder propped against the wall. The living room held more paint buckets, brushes, drop cloths and assorted tools than furniture.

She waved him to the sofa after removing a cardboard box containing paint rollers and a plastic tray. "It's cold in here," she said. "Why don't you put one of the logs in the fireplace? I'll bring us something to drink. I've got beer and colas."

"Beer's good."

She went into the kitchen and came back a second later. "I should have told you. It's not alcoholic beer."

He stared at her. "There's another kind?"

"Yes, and it tastes much better," she said, laughing. "Want to give it a try?"

"Sure." He watched her leave. Everything about this woman was just a little out of the ordinary. Even the firewood wasn't firewood, but one of those artificial logs wrapped in paper. He placed it on the fireplace grate, found a matchbox on the mantel and lit the paper wrapping below the arrows.

Lori soon brought out two amber bottles and, seeing him sitting on the hearth, placed one bottle in front of him. "All my glasses were jelly jars at one time, so I figured you'd prefer to have it straight from the bottle."

He laughed. He'd been right. Everything about Lori came with a qualifier. Yet despite that, or maybe because of it, he found himself liking her anyway. Except for those heels, there was a down-to-earth quality about her. She was who she was and made no apologies for it. That took confidence and it appealed to him.

Moments later they sat on the hearth rug in front

of the fireplace with a huge paper bowl of popcorn between them. "I see you're still using paper dinnerware," he said with a quick half smile. "Is this left over from when the kitchen was being redone?"

She shook her head. "No, actually, since I don't really know how long I'll be staying here, I try not to weigh myself down with stuff. The only exception to that rule is shoes and purses. They're my weakness."

"So you're planning on selling this place after you fix it up?"

"Hopefully, but as far as the timing goes, that'll depend on the housing market. I consider this my starter home, something that will eventually allow me to buy up."

He unscrewed the top off his bottle and did the same for hers. After taking a cautious sip, he smiled. "Hey, this is pretty good."

"It's low in calories and tastes better than regular beer. It's brewed from barley and hops, but hasn't been fermented. Think of it as nonalcoholic young beer, or wheat soda."

"It's smooth." He went to the window and, standing to the side and out of view, looked toward the street. It was quiet and no one was lurking about outside. Satisfied, he returned to where they were sitting.

"Did you hear something?"

He noticed the way she gripped the bottle. Her

knuckles were pearly-white. "No. Everything's fine, just as it should be."

"Good," she said, relieved. Lori looked at her bottle, lost in thought, then spoke. "I really should take the plunge and buy at least two matching beer steins."

"So your clothing budget trumps anything in the domesticity department?"

"Yeah, but there's a reason for that." Lori paused, as if trying to find the right words. "I can pack my clothes in several suitcases and be ready to go at a moment's notice, but it's different when it comes to household things. Some people equate filling every nook and cranny of their homes with security. I find that…constricting. Too many possessions can slow you down."

"It sounds to me like you're in a hurry to get someplace, or maybe just restless."

Lori shook her head, her expression serious. "Neither. My life is in transition, that's all. I'm searching for something that'll give me a sense of purpose, that'll make me greet each morning with a smile, or maybe just renewed determination." She sighed. "It's hard to put into words, but until I figure things out, I want to make sure my options stay open." She glanced over at him. "What about you?"

"I'm where I want to be," he said. "I'm a rancher, and though the days are long and the work's hard, it's what I was meant to do."

"I envy you. You have what I'm searching for," she said.

"A ranch?"

"No, your life's passion. You've found your place in life, so your work is the embodiment of who you are."

As they talked, time slipped by. After about an hour, a patrolman came by and took their statements. Unfortunately, the officer couldn't offer any hope that he'd be able to do much more than file the report. Without a positive ID, the department had no evidence to go on.

After the officer left, Gene could see how the interview had worn Lori down. He stayed with her until he was sure she'd be okay, then looked at his watch. It was shortly after ten. It surprised him to see how quickly the evening had gone.

Gene gave her his cell number. "Call me if you run into any more problems. I'm staying at my brother Preston's apartment while I'm in town on business."

"Then back to the ranch?"

He smiled and nodded. "Maybe you could visit me there someday. It's a real special place."

As they said good-night at the door, their eyes met. The power of that one look shot through him like a bolt of lightning. He was aware of everything about her. He heard the catch in her breath and saw her breathing quicken. When she used the tip of her tongue to moisten her lips, he nearly groaned.

He wasn't an impulsive man. He tested the water before diving in, but the temptation was too great to resist. He reached out to pull her to him, but instead of yielding, she suddenly stood on tiptoes and gave him a light kiss on the cheek.

"Good night, Gene, and thank you so much for all your help," she said softly. "If you ever need a friend, you can count on me."

"I'll see you again, Lori." Even as he spoke he knew it wasn't an idle promise. Something inside told him that he would, and sooner than either of them expected.

As she turned on the porch light and closed the door behind him, he started down the path to his truck. He'd gone only about ten feet when he caught a glimpse of movement off to his left.

It was probably just someone's stray cat, judging from the barking dog next door, but he needed to make sure. Stopping, he reached into his pocket and pretended to be searching for his keys.

Although he never turned his head, his focus was on the bushes by the house. Next door, the neighbor's dog continued to growl and bark, its head popping up intermittently as it jumped up and down just beyond the block wall.

A second later Gene saw the bushes beneath one of the windows sway slightly, odd because the breeze had died down after sunset. Uncertain of the threat, he took a few things out of his pocket, glanced down at his hand, then, as if he'd forgotten something, headed back to her door.

Gene walked slowly, furtively, studying the ground to his left in the glow of the yellow porch light. The footprints on the sandy earth didn't belong to an animal, and were too large to belong to Lori. If he'd had to take a guess, he would have said they belonged to a size ten or eleven boot—not his own size twelve.

Gene knocked on her front door and Lori answered almost instantly. "Couldn't stay away?" she said with a teasing smile.

"What can I say? You're great company," he said, laughing, then leaned over and whispered in her ear. "Don't react, just go call the police. You've got a trespasser out here beside the house."

Lori pulled him inside. "Come back in," she said, shutting the door behind him.

"Don't worry," he said quickly. "I've got this covered. I'm going to slip out your back door and go after the guy. Keep the kitchen lights off and call the police."

"*Are you crazy?* You don't know what you might be up against. He could be armed! Wait here with me for the police."

"I'll surprise him before he even knows I'm coming. Stay here."

Gene opened the door a crack and slipped outside. He knew how to move through the shadows without making a sound. *Hosteen* Silver had said that his ability was the natural result of always being in harmony with his surroundings. He wasn't sure about that, but he knew he was a match for whoever was out there sneaking around.

As Gene slipped around the far corner of the house he heard a low scraping sound. He waited, peering into the darkness, allowing his eyes to adjust. Despite the long gray shadows, he could see a shape huddled below the window directly ahead.

Gene moved toward the man cautiously, scarcely breathing and carefully placing each footstep to avoid making any noise. In the muted half-light, he could see the figure ahead. From the sheen and flattened appearance of his face, it was obvious the person was wearing a stocking mask. He could see something in his gloved hand, too, some kind of tool. It was probably a screwdriver, undoubtedly intended to help the intruder pry the window open.

Gene moved even closer, then stopped, hearing slow footsteps behind him. Nobody had ever been able to successfully sneak up on him—that was one skill he'd had as far back as he could remember. More than once, as a kid, that ability had helped him avoid getting beaten up by a bully.

He flattened against the wall of the house, farther into the shadows. A second later, Lori appeared, crouched low and holding something in her hand.

He grabbed her and covered her mouth with his hand as he pulled her toward him.

She slammed her elbow into his gut.

"Be still. It's me," he whispered.

The intruder must have also heard, because quick footsteps sounded up ahead.

Gene placed himself between her and the intruder just as something came flying in his direction. Gene blocked the object with his forearm, and it bounced off the house with a loud thud. It was the screwdriver.

"Wait here," Gene told Lori, then took off after the running man, who'd now ducked around to the front of the house.

As Gene raced around the corner, the fleeing man stumbled over a lawn sprinkler and nearly lost his balance. Seeing Gene closing in, he grabbed a rake from the neighbor's yard and hurled it at him.

Gene dodged, but it slowed him down, and when he looked up, the man had reached a car parked on the opposite side of the street. Before Gene could narrow the distance separating them, the guy raced off and Gene had no chance to read the plates.

Gene cursed as he stared at the fading taillights. If Lori hadn't come outside and tipped the guy off, he would have had him for sure. He was crossing back across the street when Lori came out toward him, holding a mop handle in one hand and a flashlight in the other.

"I wish you'd stayed inside," Gene said, his voice calm now. It was no use getting riled up after the fact. "He heard you coming and spooked."

"I won't abandon a friend and you were out here

alone. I grabbed the closest thing I had to a weapon, and came to help you."

The tremor in her voice sliced through what was left of his anger. Although she'd been terrified, she'd risked her own safety to help him. The gesture was touching. With the exception of his foster family, no one had ever done that.

Lori was unpredictable, but she had heart. As he looked at her, he felt the tug in his gut—and lower.

"Give me the flashlight, then stay close behind me," he said, forcing his thoughts back on to safer channels. "I want to take a look around, but I don't want you out of my sight again."

"The police are on their way," she said.

"Good. Just give me some room. I want to figure out what he was up to out here," he said, walking back to the house.

Using the flashlight, and careful not to obliterate any footprints, he studied the gouges on the window.

Next, he aimed the flashlight beam toward the ground and quickly located the screwdriver. Hoping there was still a chance of recovering the man's fingerprints, he left it on the ground and backed away.

"He tried to pry that window open," he said, pointing. "What's on the other side?"

"My bedroom," she whispered in a shaky voice.

Chapter Four

A tired-looking police officer, Sergeant Elroy Chavez, responded to the call ten minutes later. Gene filled him in.

"You didn't touch anything, right?" Sergeant Chavez asked.

"No. I figured you'd want to check for prints, but I should warn you, the guy was wearing gloves," Gene said.

"You sure it was a man?" Chavez pressed.

Gene nodded. "I saw his shape and the way he ran."

"It's got to be Bud Harrington," Lori said, looking at both men and trying hard to appear calm. Inside, she felt as if she were unraveling a little at a time. "The creep's playing with my head, hoping to make me too scared to even go home."

She and Gene stayed well back as the sergeant collected whatever evidence he could find and took a few photos. "This is all I can do here right now." Sergeant Chavez looked at her, then added, "I'd advise you to stay somewhere else for a few days, or find someone to keep watch. The few officers we have available are working double shifts and dealing with a lot of extra calls. On top of that, our detectives are up to their necks investigating an organized gang of identity thieves working our area. We're overworked at every level, so response times are really slow. You're just lucky the guy didn't wait until you'd gone to sleep."

She swallowed hard. "I'll get an alarm."

"If it's personal, that might just make him angrier, and still not be enough in the long run," Sergeant Chavez said. "We'll have extra patrols in the area tonight, but you really should consider making arrangements to stay elsewhere, at least for a while."

"This wasn't the work of a pro. If it had been, he wouldn't have left one of his tools behind and risk having it somehow traced back to him," Gene said, thinking out loud. "Taken at face value, what happened tonight makes no sense. A burglar would have waited until no one was home, or Ms. Baker was asleep. At the very least, it would have made a lot more sense to wait until after I'd left."

"Maybe he didn't know you were still here, but either way, none of that lessens the threat. Give some serious consideration to what I suggested," he said, looking back at Lori.

As Sergeant Chavez walked away, Lori's heart was hammering and her mouth was dry. Fear pounded through her with each beat of her heart. She had absolutely no idea what to do now.

"Would you like me to stick around for a few more hours?"

"Do you think he'll come back tonight to try and finish what he started?" Her voice rose and her throat tightened.

"Normally, I'd say no, but this guy doesn't act in a way that makes sense to me. That makes him unpredictable."

"I won't be getting much sleep tonight," she said softly.

"So you're not going to take the officer's advice and move out for a while?"

"Move where? How can I possibly justify staying at a friend's, knowing I could be leading danger right to their doorstep? I could go to a motel, but I'll be endangering others there, as well." She took a shaky breath. "But it's more than that. Allowing fear to dictate what you do is never a good thing. You lose a piece of yourself when you do that. Can you understand?"

He nodded. "I hear you."

As they stood by his truck, she glanced at his rifle, hung on a rack and locked in place in the cab. "How about letting me rent that from you for a few days?"

"It's got a powerful kick. Do you think you can handle it?" He unlocked the rack and took it down. "It's a Winchester .30-30. It's accurate up to a couple hundred yards. Have you ever handled one before?"

"No, but how hard can it be? Point the barrel and pull the trigger. Just show me how to put bullets in it."

He shook his head. "No, forget that. If you've never used one, you won't be able to handle it, especially if you're frightened. You're more likely to have it taken away and used against you. Maybe someday I can bring you to my ranch and show you how to shoot, but without any training you're far more likely to hurt yourself or a neighbor. Bullets travel far and have a way of hitting unintended targets. That's why rifles, by and large, are too dangerous in urban areas."

"Yeah, you're right," she said. "I need to think of something else."

As she looked at him she had to bite back a sigh. She would have loved hiring him as a guard. Gene was tall, his shoulders broad, his chest muscular. Having a man like him beside her would have practically guaranteed the safety of everything but her heart.

Nothing about Gene was ordinary. His skin was the color of warm caramel, but it was his dark eyes that attracted her the most. Despite his strength, they mirrored only gentleness.

Trying to focus on something safer, she pointed to the braided leather bridle that hung on a hook in the back of the pickup's cab. "That's beautiful."

"That belongs to Grit, my brother Paul's horse. Our foster father left the animal to him. Grit's a handful, and Paul's as stubborn as they come, so those two have a minor war going on now. In all fairness, Grit doesn't make life easy for anyone. I left the bridle too close to his stall, so he bit through it. I had to have a section replaced."

"It sounds like he's going to take careful handling."

"Grit has problems," he said, nodding. "So far, I'm the only one who can ride him. Grit's an old rodeo horse that was about to be sold to a slaughterhouse when my foster father found him. *Hosteen* Silver never had a problem with Grit, but the horse wouldn't accept any other rider, not without a showdown."

"You're good with horses, I take it?"

"For the most part, yeah," he said without any false modesty. "Horses, like people, have different temperaments. Each one requires individual attention. Grit enjoys hassling my brothers and me," he said. "It's like a game for him."

"I love animals. I don't know where my life's going to eventually lead me, but I'm sure of one thing. Animals are going to be part of the picture." She wanted the conversation to continue forever. She liked hearing him talk and didn't want him to go.

As they stood by his truck, Lori noticed Gene's own reluctance to say good-night. Looking into his eyes, she realized that he was worried about her. The knowledge sent a pleasant rush of warmth through her.

"It's really getting late. You better call it a day. I'll be fine," she said at last. "Sergeant Chavez promised extra patrols in the area."

"Stay away from the windows and keep my phone number handy. I'm just a call and probably fifteen minutes away."

Lori went back inside and made sure the door was locked and bolted. Still scared, she went into the kitchen, and taking an armful of pots and pans, stacked them near the windows and the doors. If anyone tried to break in, the pans would fall and make a dreadful racket. That would buy her time to run, or hide and call the police.

Lastly, she took her large butcher knife out of the silverware drawer. She'd be sleeping with that, her flashlight and the cell phone beside her pillow tonight.

As she went into the bedroom, her thoughts drifted back to Gene. Would it have killed her to invite him to spend the night? A man like that would not only have kept the intruder away, he would have made each hour an adventure to remember.

Yet even as the thought formed, she laughed. Casual intimacy just wasn't her style. Her heart's needs required more than a few hours of passion. For her, it would have to be all or nothing.

Her mother and father had gone from the perfect marriage to divorce—from love to hate. The shock of learning they were splitting up, and the painful aftermath, had left its scars. She'd never settle for the kind of love that came with requirements, boundaries or time limits.

She wanted it all and was willing to wait however long it took to find it.

GENE DROVE AWAY FROM THE house slowly. There was something about Lori Baker that had definitely gotten under his skin. Though she was afraid, she'd still managed to reach down into herself and find the courage not to back down. That alone was worthy of his respect, but there was a lot more to Lori than just that. From the first moment he'd laid eyes on her, he'd been drawn to her. She was a beauty, and the way she looked at him made him want to take on an army to keep her safe.

He'd spent a lot of years as the underdog and knew the pain and frustration it brought. The fact that he'd been the skinniest runt in the foster home had made him fair game to the bullies, and he'd been on the losing end of a lot of fights growing up.

Time had changed all that. Now he was over six feet tall, as strong as a bull and could stack seventy-pound bales of hay all day, if that's what he had to do. Work had built up his muscles and he could hold his own in any fight.

Tonight he'd equalized the odds against her, but something continued to nag at him. Making a spur-of-the-moment decision, something rare for him, he pulled over to the curb and called his brother Paul. "So what do you think?" he asked after updating him.

"The incidents could be related, bro, but what the heck are you doing getting involved in all that? No, wait—let me guess. She's hot?"

"Man, you've got a one-track mind. Why can't she be an ordinary lady who happened to ask for help?"

"Because you're still worried about her. Face it, bro. Up till now, the only females you've been interested in have had manes and tails," Paul said. "So she must be something special. What's the lady's name?"

"Planning on doing a background check?"

"Hey, you called *me* for advice, so let me do what I do," he said. "Tell me everything you know about her."

As Gene spoke, he could hear Paul typing away at his keyboard.

"Okay, I've got a description and address on that Bud Harrington guy. He's five foot eleven, one hundred sixty-five pounds," he said, then read off the address. "Drive by his house and see if anything in particular catches your eye, like a familiar vehicle. Just don't go poking inside private property or I may have to bail your butt out of jail."

Gene drove up the well-lit neighborhood street twenty minutes later. Bud Harrington's house appeared to be an unremarkable, middle-class split-level home. The front had a well-tended lawn and several mature trees. For a home in town, it wasn't half-bad.

Slowing down to look things over carefully, Gene noted that the porch light and a front room lamp were both on. He could also see at least three newspapers thrown on the porch, and letters and flyers sticking out of the mailbox. A late-model blue pickup was parked in the driveway, but judging from the leaves atop the cab and a tumbleweed jammed under the rear axle, it probably hadn't been driven recently.

It was time to call it a day. He'd avoided going to his brother Preston's apartment long enough. He hated downtime whenever he was away from the ranch because that's when he'd start thinking of all the chores that needed doing back home.

Tonight was different. He'd have other things to occupy his thoughts. Lori Baker remained at the edges of his mind, tantalizingly out of his reach. He shook his head. The real problem was that he hadn't had a woman in his life for far too long. That, all by itself, could scramble a man's thinking. His life lacked balance.

GENE AWOKE TO SUNLIGHT playing on his face. He stretched, working the kinks out. He'd fallen asleep on the sofa, his legs on the coffee table, watching TV. He must have been more tired than he'd thought. As he got up, ready to undress and shower, his phone rang. He reached over and lifted it off the coffee table

"Hey, you awake, farm boy?" Paul said. "I've got some interesting information for you. Why don't you come over to my place?"

Twenty minutes later Gene picked up four breakfast burritos from the Hen House up on Twentieth Street, then drove over to Paul's.

They emptied the sack of food on the kitchen counter, loaded up their plates, then stepped over to the small dining table. A laptop lay open on one side and Paul took the seat by it.

"Are you sure Lori Baker's worth all this trouble? There are a lot of unattached ladies out there, bro."

"She needs a little backup right now. She's getting picked on by someone who doesn't fight fair, and I've never had a lot of patience with bullies," Gene said.

"Okay, let's see what I can do for you." He went into the next room, then came back with a small leather case. "Here. It's a photo ID I made up for you. Take it. It may come in handy."

"Grayhorse Investigations," he said, opening it. "So I'm a consultant for your P.I. firm?"

"Anytime you decide to give up ranching, you can come work for me."

"Don't hold your breath," he said.

Paul sat down by his computer and typed for a moment before looking up. "Harrington's bad news when it comes to women. Last month the police broke up a fight between him and the very protective father of a twenty-year-old college cheerleader he kept hounding for a date. Though Harrington could have pressed for assault, he apparently wasn't big on making it an issue, either."

"He definitely sounds like the stalker type, but I drove by his house and it looks like he hasn't been there for several days. His pickup hasn't moved for at least that long. Of course it's possible he has a car or another home here in town, or maybe a girlfriend."

"Nothing I could find," Paul said. "I'll tell you what. Bring the ID I gave you and let's go have a chat with his neighbors, see what else we can find out about him."

Gene hesitated. "You shouldn't be out in the field yet, not with that gimpy shoulder of yours. If we run into a problem…"

"You can handle it," Paul said with a wide grin. "I'll stand back and keep score."

Gene choked on his coffee. "Like you could actually stay out of any street fight."

"We'll find out. Let's go. You drive."

Chapter Five

Lori went to work early the following morning, hoping that if Bud Harrington was around, he'd show up too late to follow her.

Her supervisor, Jerry Esteban, would probably be thrilled to see her come in early instead of right under the wire. Punching in the entry code on the keypad lock, Lori let herself into the building using the back door and went straight to the break room. Her best friend, Miranda Hoff, was already there, sitting at the table eating a glazed doughnut.

Seeing Lori, she smiled. "Busted. I came in early so I could eat my doughnuts in peace."

Lori laughed. "Charlie's still after you to stay on that health food diet?"

She patted her huge belly. "The baby will be here in six weeks, and since he knows how much I love junk food he's watched over me like a hawk." She made a face. "If I see one more fruit smoothie or those green health food shakes of his, I may scream and traumatize our offspring."

Lori laughed.

"But why on earth are *you* here so early?" Miranda asked, eyes narrowed.

Lori filled her in, and then ended the story by telling her about Gene. "He really stood up for me when it mattered."

"Are we talking the tall Indian man with the cowboy hat who was at your window late yesterday afternoon?"

"You noticed?"

"I'm pregnant, not dead," she said with a sly smile. "It's like I've always said, the bad things in life often lead to something good."

"You're the eternal optimist," Lori said.

Miranda looked at the clock. "Time to get out there. I wanted to clean up my workstation before we open."

Lori watched her friend walk away. She envied Miranda. Charlie adored her, and Miranda was crazy about him in return. Now they were expecting their first baby.

She wondered if she'd ever find the focused, purpose-driven life she craved. Time marched on, and with each day that came, her hopes seemed to vanish under the glare of the morning sun.

Lori walked out into the main office and saw Steve Farmer, her coworker, and Harvey Bishop, their security man, sipping cups of coffee and watching people already gathering by the entrance. In five minutes Harvey would be opening the doors.

A man in a cowboy hat was standing just outside,

and Lori thought about Gene, wondering when she'd see him again. On impulse, she decided to call his cell and invite him out to lunch today. She wasn't the kind to sit idly by a silent phone wishing and hoping. The direct approach was more her style.

GENE AND PAUL WALKED DOWN the sidewalk toward Gene's truck after talking to the last resident on Harrington's block. "You really should consider a career as a P.I., bro. People open up to you without even thinking about it," Paul said.

"No, that wasn't it. Harrington's neighbors don't like him very much, and they're hoping someone will drive him out of town."

As he slipped behind the wheel of his truck, Gene's phone rang. He picked it up and smiled as he heard Lori's voice. "Where and when?" he asked seconds later.

When he hung up, Gene noticed the odd way Paul was looking at him. "Let me guess," Paul said. "That was Lori?"

"Yeah, she wants to meet for lunch. She's buying."

"You've got it bad, bro. I hate to break it to you, but you're going down," Paul said, shaking his head.

LORI DROVE TO SIMPLE Pleasures, looking forward to lunch with Gene at her favorite Hartley restaurant. Though it was across town, the drive was well worth it.

Realizing she was early, Lori asked to be seated at a booth by the front window. She could watch for Gene from there.

As she glanced up and down the street looking for Gene's pickup, she spotted a maroon van parked on the south side of the restaurant.

The driver got out and Lori held her breath. He was wearing a baseball cap, sunglasses and a Scorpions windbreaker. Absolutely certain that it was Harrington again, she reached for her cell phone and called the police.

"Has he made any threatening moves or tried to approach you?" the dispatcher asked.

"No, Harrington's just standing there by his van, probably waiting for me to come back outside."

"Stay inside the restaurant. You should be safe there. We'll have an officer on the scene in twenty minutes. If anything changes, call back immediately."

Frustrated, Lori closed the phone and leaned closer to the window, trying to get a better look at the man outside. It had to be Bud Harrington, but she couldn't figure out why he was doing this to her.

Trying to follow the dispatcher's instructions, she fought the urge to go outside and confront him once and for all. Yet it was such a busy street. What could he possibly do to her out in the open?

She started to get out of her seat, then sat back down. She'd need to warn Gene to stay away. Afterward, she'd go. Lori reached for her cell phone, called and told Gene what was happening. "Don't come over. I'll buy you lunch some other time. I've already been in touch with the police and there might be trouble."

"Is he still out there?"

"Yeah, and I'm going to go have it out with him. He's not going to attack me right beside a crowded street and I'm tired of this nonsense."

"Stay where you are. Busy street or not, you can't be sure what he's going to do," Gene said. "What did the police say their response time would be?"

"Twenty minutes."

"I'm less than five minutes away. Let me handle this. I can hold him there for the police."

GENE HAD JUST BEEN ABOUT to leave Paul's apartment when Lori's call came in. Placing the phone back in his jacket pocket, he gave his brother a quick update.

"Give me a chance to call my client and reschedule my morning meeting," Paul said. "Then I'll go with you."

"It's not necessary. If it's the same guy I saw last night, I won't have a problem."

Paul, already on the phone, muttered a curse when he got put on hold. "All right, go. I'm going to need my own vehicle, so I'll head your way in a few minutes."

Gene ran to his pickup and drove away, mentally planning the quickest route to Simple Pleasures.

He made good time and all the lights, right up

to the last intersection. When he stopped at the red light just down the block from Simple Pleasures, he saw the maroon van she'd described. A guy wearing a blue cap and a dark hooded sweatshirt with the Scorpions logo was leaning against the driver's door.

The distinctive clatter of Gene's big diesel engine made the man glance casually up the street. The second he spotted Gene's truck the guy jumped into the van, and in a matter of seconds, the van had backed out of the slot and was on the move.

Pinned in by the cars ahead, beside and behind him, there was no way Gene could get through the intersection before the light changed.

Just then Paul called and Gene put the phone on speaker.

"He's in the van now, heading toward the north end of the parking lot," Gene said. "Where are you?"

"Coming up from behind," Paul said. "I see you. I'll go straight. You take the right turn and cut through the parking lot just in case he decides to turn east."

"Gotcha." Gene made a quick right, then a left into the front of the restaurant lot. Ahead, he could see the van cutting back left, right out into the street. Paul was now in the best position.

Gene had slowed for a stop sign when Lori suddenly rushed up and jumped onto the passenger-side running board.

"Let me in," Lori shouted, tugging at the door handle.

He hit the button and the lock clicked open.

Lori jumped in, then scrambled for her shoulder belt.

"What is it with you and moving cars, woman? You're an accident waiting to happen," he snapped.

"Later. Let's catch him before he gets away."

Gene concentrated on his driving. He took the same route as the van, entered the next parallel street, then whipped left.

"I can't see him anymore. There are too many cars," Lori said, straining to see ahead.

"I've got him." Paul's voice came from the phone on the console. "He just passed through Ellison, still heading north. He's in the center lane."

"Great!" Lori said, looking down at the phone. "Gene, you didn't tell me you were bringing backup."

"No, *Gene*'s the backup," Paul said over the speaker. "I'm the closest you've got to law enforcement here. You two are civilians, don't forget that."

Gene didn't argue, focusing solely on closing the gap between him and Lori's stalker and trying to beat the next light.

"Keep left, and I'll take the right lane," Paul said. "Whichever way he cuts, one of us will be in position to stay on his tail."

"Done." Gene raced along, sometimes throwing Lori back into the seat despite the shoulder harness and seat belt as he whipped around slower vehicles. Over the speaker, they could also hear Paul's engine racing and tires squealing.

Gene could see the van now, as well as Paul's Jeep. As he watched, Paul closed in.

The van ran a red light, barely missing a white utility truck. The utility truck driver, who'd spun the wheel trying to dodge a direct hit, came to a screeching stop. Gene had to stand on his brakes to keep from rear-ending a two-seater sedan not much bigger than a riding mower.

"Forget it. We're screwed," Paul said at last. "Traffic is snarled up here and I can't get through."

More vehicles entered the intersection on the cross street. All were forced to a screeching stop because the utility truck's sudden maneuver had sent its ladder flying into the middle of the street.

"There goes Harrington," Lori said, pointing. The van, now at the top of a low hill, disappeared to the east around a wide curve. "Can we turn right and cut him off?"

Gene looked over at her, then at the two full lanes of back-to-back vehicles on her side. "No way."

"So he's gone again," she said softly, and leaned back in her seat.

"Paul, did you get a look at the plates?"

"I only got a partial, but I'm running the few numbers I've got against Harrington," he said, then, after a beat, continued. "Looks like that plate might belong on his Ford pickup. Harrington doesn't own a van."

"Harrington had a blue pickup in his driveway," Gene said. "But something doesn't make sense here. Why would Harrington bother to switch the plates onto that van? The van didn't point directly to him, but the plate does."

"It doesn't make any sense to me, either," Paul said.

"I guess I might as well buy you lunch," Lori said with a shaky smile. "You, too, Paul."

"Not yet. We need to report this to the police. Let's head over to the station. We'll back up your statement, Lori," Paul said.

"Afterward, we eat," Lori said. "You guys have been terrific."

"I'll have to pass on that lunch invitation," Paul said. "I've got to meet a client as soon as we're done at the station."

"Then it'll be just you and me, Gene," she said.

"Works for me," he said, and smiled.

Chapter Six

They were seated inside a small office at the police station, preparing to sign their statements. Sergeant Chavez, waiting with them for the clerk to reappear, offered them coffee.

"Isn't there any way you can arrest Harrington?" Lori asked, accepting the offered foam cup.

"Not on the basis of what you've given us," Chavez said. "There weren't any fingerprints on that screwdriver, either. Face it, Ms. Baker. You still haven't been able to make a positive ID. One of our officers stopped by to interview Harrington, but no one was at home. We'll keep trying."

"It's *got* to be him. He's the only person I've had a problem with at the DMV. I grew up in this community, and I've lived a very quiet life. Most of the time if I'm not on the job, I'm working on my home. It's a fixer-upper."

"What about old boyfriends?" Paul said.

"I date on occasion, but not regularly. It's been at least six months since I went out on a date," she said. "That's why I keep saying that it has to be Bud Harrington. His body type and clothing fit, too."

"That's not conclusive evidence, Ms. Baker," Chavez said.

"But the absence of any other possibility—" she said.

"Is still not evidence," Chavez said, finishing her thought. "We spoke to the suspect after your first complaint and you know how that came out. He claimed he was the injured party."

Lori took a sip of the hot, bitter coffee, then stood and began to pace. "I'm not sure what else I can do. This isn't going to just go away."

"You need to seriously consider taking my advice. Get out of town for a while," Chavez said. "Whoever's after you is getting bolder, and that's not a good sign."

Just then a clerk came into the room and placed the typed statements before Sergeant Chavez.

Chavez handed them their statements. "Read them over carefully and then sign."

When they were done, Chavez took the forms. "I'll follow up on this and take it as far as I can," he told Lori. "Just don't expect miracles. You've given me very little evidence to go on."

"There's the question of how the license plate that belongs on Harrington's pickup got on that van," Paul said. "Is there any way you can stake out Harrington's home?"

Chavez shook his head. "We don't have the manpower right now. No one's life is in immediate danger, so it's not going to be given a high priority," Chavez said. "I wish things were different, but they are what they are."

As Paul, Gene and Lori left the building and walked out into the parking lot, Paul spoke. "I have to get on a flight to D.C. tonight and meet with my former boss. The Marshals Service has requested that I review some new evidence that's turned up on my last case."

"Do they have a lead on who ordered the hit on the federal judge?" Gene asked.

"I'm not sure. I wasn't given any details on the phone. I'll know more when I meet with my district marshal," he said. "I'll probably be gone for a day, maybe two, so try to stay out of trouble."

"We'll do our best to manage without you," Gene said in a labored voice, then flashed Paul a teasing grin.

"Do me a favor. Just don't do anything stupid," Paul growled.

After Paul left, Gene and Lori walked out to Gene's pickup. "Do you want me to drive you back to your car, or straight to work?" Gene asked.

"I asked for the afternoon off," she said. "What I'd really like to do now is drive by Bud's place."

"Sure. I was going to take another pass by there again anyway. Maybe Harrington's home now."

"If he's there, we can both talk to him."

"No way," Gene said.

"I can't keep running from him forever, Gene. Better that I should face him when I've got someone beside me than run into him when I'm alone."

For several long moments Gene considered what she'd said, then finally spoke after they'd climbed into his pickup. "Here's my deal. I'll take you there and stand by you if you decide you want to confront him—but if there's trouble, I want you to run back to the truck, lock yourself in and call the cops."

"I can't just leave if you—"

"My way or no way," he interrupted. "Your choice." He placed the key in the ignition but didn't start the engine.

She wanted to argue, but knew from the set of his jaw that his mind was made up. "Okay. I agree to your terms."

He got under way shortly thereafter. "What did you tell them at work?"

"The truth, though I was a little worried about doing that. I didn't want them to think I posed a danger to the others, and frighten everyone for no reason."

"How do you like working there?"

"It's a good job and I get a decent salary, but it's not what I plan to do the rest of my life."

"What kind of work would you do if you had complete freedom of choice?"

"I'm not sure. That's why I'm still looking around, exploring. All I'm one hundred percent sure about is that once I find the right place for myself, I'll know it."

"What is it that you'd like to find in a job—excitement, maybe?"

"It wouldn't exclude excitement, but it goes beyond that. What I'm really looking for is work that'll allow me to contribute something worthwhile, maybe the kind of job where I can make a difference in my own way. I'd like to know I'm doing more with my life than just using up oxygen and getting by."

"You want to know that you're working toward something, not just working. That's exactly the way I feel about my ranch," he said with a nod. "You'll find what's right for you, too, if you keep looking and refuse to give up."

As their eyes met, she felt a delicious prickle of awareness. More than anything, she wanted to get to know him better, to see the man beyond the yummy package.

Yet, although it was tempting to lower her guard, in the past, that kind of trust had led her straight to heartbreak and disappointment. Those memories were powerful enough to urge her to pull back.

Fifteen minutes later, they drove slowly past Bud Harrington's house. The newspapers and mail Gene had seen before were still on the porch. In the daylight, Gene could see that a layer of dust covered the pickup, windows included.

"Someone screwed the license plate back on the truck," he said, calling her attention to it.

"Maybe it's not the same plate," she said. "After all, Paul only saw the letters and wasn't totally sure about the numbers."

Gene stopped just behind the tailgate of the pickup. "There's no dust on the plate, unlike the truck. How else could that happen except by taking off the plate, then putting it back on?"

"But why on earth would Bud go through all that trouble? Does he think he can somehow weasel out of this by using his own plates on the wrong vehicle? Or is someone messing with *his* mind?"

"*And* yours," Gene said. "All good questions, and if he's back, why not pick up the mail and those newspapers, too? It could very well be that someone else is responsible. Keep in mind that, as near as we can tell, Harrington doesn't own a van, and the maroon one we saw didn't look like a rental. Rental vans are usually white—or black."

"So where does that leave us?" she asked.

"Right where we started. Nowhere."

She sighed. "I'm sorry I dragged you into this mess, Gene, but I'm glad you're here."

He gave her a slow smile. "I've got no regrets. I happen to like you."

She bit her bottom lip and smiled. "I don't care if that's just a line. You make it sound good."

He laughed. "It's no line, sweetheart. You're un-predictable and a bundle of trouble, but you've also got more than your share of courage and determination. You don't back down, even when you should."

She had started to answer when her phone rang. It was Miranda. "What's wrong?" she asked immediately.

"We're really shorthanded here, and Jerry wanted me to ask you if there's any way you can come back in this afternoon. I've got a doctor's appointment, so I've got to leave here soon, and we've got a real backlog," she said. "Are you still at the station?"

"No, I'm not, but tell me something. Does everyone know what happened?" Lori asked.

"Yeah, Jerry told Harvey, then us to keep an eye out for anyone acting strangely," she said. "Right now Jerry's working your window, but he has a report to finish for Santa Fe this afternoon, so he's pretty tense."

"I'll be back in fifteen minutes," she said, and hung up. At least there was a measure of job security knowing she was needed. "I have to get back to work ASAP. Can you take me to my car?"

"Sure. We're just a few minutes from the restaurant now," Gene said. "You can drive on to work from there and I'll tail you until you arrive just to make sure there are no more surprises."

"I really appreciate that, but I'm starting to feel guilty. You've been spending all your time with me, and I'm sure you've got responsibilities of your own you've been neglecting because of that."

"Do you trust me?"

The quick, blunt question took her by surprise. "Of course. You've put your own safety on the line because of me. Why on earth wouldn't I trust you?"

"All right, then," he said with an approving nod. "You remember Officer Chavez suggested you get away from home for a while?"

"Yeah, but—"

He held up one hand. "I happen to think he's right and I've got an idea. You get off work at five?" he asked.

"Thereabouts. More like five-fifteen or so."

"Okay. I'm going to be waiting outside when you get off work, but don't look for me. I'll hang back and follow you home. Then I want you to pack up a few things and come with me."

"Where to?"

"I'm staying at my brother's place. It's a small apartment, but you can have the bedroom. I'll sleep on the couch."

She shook her head slowly. "You've been really terrific, but I can't keep doing this to you. It's just not fair."

"I'm volunteering, so it's fair," he said with an easy smile. "You've met Paul, who's in law enforcement, or at least was. I've also got two more brothers who are federal agents, and then there's Preston, whose apartment we'll be using. He's a detective with the Hartley Police Department. If at any time you think I've said or done anything that's out of line, you can pick one or two of them to come arrest me."

She laughed, then, growing serious, answered, "What you're offering me is very tempting, but standing on my own two feet is also important to me."

"There are some fights that can't be won alone, Lori. Think about my offer. This really isn't a good time for a solo act."

After Gene dropped her off by her car, she drove directly to work. She wasn't sure what to do. As a kid she'd learned the hard way to rely only on herself, especially after her parents' divorce. The bitterness between them had left her caught up in the middle. She'd learned to look only to herself for help since no one else was there for her. Those lessons had come at a high price and explained at least partially why close relationships made her uncomfortable. She'd worked hard to become independent, but, now, this new situation was forcing her hand.

Lori entered the DMV building, nodded to Harvey, the security guard, then walked across the room to her window, where Jerry now sat.

"I'm glad you're back," he said. "Before you get started, I'd like to have a word with you. Come to my office, please."

Lori followed the tall, shaved-headed man in his mid-fifties down the hall and into his small office.

"Take a seat," Jerry said, then shut the door behind them. "I've heard about your continuing problem with Mr. Harrington. I've already alerted security, but I need to know if he may pose a danger to anyone else in this office."

"No, he won't. He's focused on me, but I should tell you that I have no proof my stalker really is Bud Harrington," she said.

Jerry leaned back in his chair. "This office has had problems with Harrington before, especially during a time when he was selling off a car collection and had to conduct business here frequently. On the surface, he's a respectable jewelry maker, the owner of Harrington Designs, but the guy's nuts. He gave one of our former clerks a hard time by harassing her at her window, but it never went any further than that. Security escorted him out."

"I hadn't heard about that."

"I told the police all about it when they called earlier. It happened before your time here. Ann King, a former employee, had problems with him. It was nothing more than off-color remarks, but the second time, Steve Farmer was working the window next to hers and overheard him. He waved over a security guard, who threatened to hold him for the police. There were no more problems after that."

"Then it looks like Harrington's behavior went down a notch or two," she said, and updated him.

"So he's learned to disguise his identity," Jerry said slowly. "Do you have any doubt that it's Harrington?"

"Not in my own mind, but I also have no proof, so the police can't arrest him."

Jerry considered it silently, steepling his fingers and staring down at his hands, deep in thought. "I want you to keep me informed," he said, then stood. "You know I'm about to go on vacation, but I can switch around the dates if there's a chance you're going to need a leave of absence."

"I don't foresee that. He's no threat to me here with all the people around and Harvey on guard."

"All right, then. Let's get back to work and see if we can process everyone by closing."

It was late afternoon and Lori was working at her window when she finally decided to take the next step on her own. If she confronted Harrington, put it on the line by telling him that she knew he was the one stalking her, maybe he'd stop playing these crazy games—or at least back off for a while.

Fifteen minutes later, Lori closed her window. As her break started, she found the telephone number for Harrington Designs in the phone book, reached for her desk phone, then stopped. Calling him from here was a bad idea. Harrington's caller ID would show the origin and he might use it to get her into trouble. She didn't want to give up her cell phone number, either.

Lori walked to the lobby. Mounted on the wall was one of the few landline public phones in the area.

She inserted two quarters and dialed the number,

trying to figure out the best way to say what she needed.

"Harrington Designs, where custom-designed jewelry is our specialty," he announced cheerfully. "This is Bud."

"Harrington, if you don't leave me alone, the next person you're going to see at your door is a police detective," she said. "I know it's you following me around and I'm tired of your games. You're not scaring me, you're just pissing me off. So stop wasting your time and mine."

"Um, you clearly have the wrong number. Who is this?"

"You know exactly who this is, Bud. You hounded me at my workplace, lied to the police and now you're stalking me. There are laws against that, so be warned. If I even *think* I see you again, I'll file stalking charges. I'm keeping a record of all this, and you're going to spend some time in jail."

"Ah, now I know who you are. Lori something, the woman from the Department of Motor Vehicles who just can't stand rejection. Hey, lady, speaking of evidence, I'm recording this call now, and if you don't stop bothering me, I'll have *your* job. Don't make me have to hire a lawyer and saddle you with a restraining order. Get a life."

He hung up and Lori stood there, shaking, not out of fear but out of anger. Taking a deep breath, she put the phone back on the receiver. That's when she saw the elderly man barely five feet away. He'd probably come in while she'd been talking to Harrington. He stood there, watching her.

"You okay, miss?" he asked.

Quickly putting on her game face, she nodded and smiled. "I'm fine, sir. A little personal issue, that's all."

"Okay, then," the gray-haired gentleman said.

As he walked past her, Lori turned to look out into the parking lot. A pickup went by on the street outside hauling a horse trailer, and she noted the two cowboys in the cab, judging from their hats.

Ranchers and cowboys.... That made her think of Gene and she smiled. It was impossible not to be drawn to him. The way he'd protected her touched her heart. He was helping her of his own free will. Nothing was compelling him...except maybe the magic between them. Whenever they were together, excitement was thick in the air, the kind that had nothing to do with the danger trailing her.

Yet no matter how strong the sparks between them were, she knew he'd have to return to his ranch soon. After that...she'd probably never see him again.

Lori sighed. Trying to figure out the future was an exercise in futility. For now, she had an ally. Tomorrow would have to take care of itself.

IT WAS FIVE-TWENTY BY THE time Lori left the building and walked to her car. She noticed Gene's truck at the far end of the parking lot but made it a point not to look in that direction as he'd asked.

Fifteen minutes later she arrived home and drove up her driveway. By the time she parked, Gene was walking up to meet her. "I didn't see the maroon van anywhere. Did you?" she asked.

"No, but he knows where you live. You really shouldn't stay here tonight," he said.

"I'm going to pull my car into the garage, then let's go into the house and talk," she said.

A few minutes later she led the way through an interior garage door into the kitchen. "I really love this house," she said. After a beat she added, "Maybe 'cause it's mine."

"I hear you," he said with a knowing smile. "Two Springs Ranch is far from perfect—there's always a fence that needs fixing or an irrigation ditch waiting to be cleaned out, and the bunkhouse still needs a lot of work—but I love it there. I wake up every morning raring to get to work. That ranch is my present and my future."

"Is there a future Mrs. Redhouse on the horizon?"

He laughed. "No, I'm nowhere near ready to settle down. I still have a lot of plans for my place, and until those get off the ground, I won't have the time it takes to build a relationship with anyone."

"So what brought you into town?"

"Paperwork—mostly legal issues that need straightening out. Our foster father passed away recently and there are things that still need to be done."

"I'm so sorry for your loss." Seeing him nod stiffly, then look away, Lori dropped the subject. It was clear to her that he didn't want to talk further about it, and she didn't want to make him uncomfortable.

Instead, she told him about looking up Harrington's business in the phone book, and her short conversation with him. "His denial was predictable," she said with a shrug. "I really wish the police would just catch Bud in the act and throw his butt in jail. I hate the thought of some jerk running me out of my own home, even if it's just temporary."

"I could stay here with you tonight, but one of us would have to be awake at all times, and exhaustion might eventually turn us into easy targets," he said. "All things considered, staying here is a particularly bad strategy right now. Your call might have motivated him to do something even more reckless."

"All right," Lori said. "Let me get a few things together. Then I'd like to tell my neighbor, Mrs. Hopgood, that I'm going to be away, and if she sees anyone hanging around, she should call the police."

"Excellent idea."

Chapter Seven

A half hour later they were driving across town in Gene's truck, an overly large suitcase behind them on the rear seat of the extended cab.

"I'm glad you packed for several days," he said.

"Actually, I bring this much along with me even on overnight trips. I've never been the type of savvy traveler who can make do with one of those itty-bitty travel carryalls. I can't fit everything I need into them. It would cost a fortune for me to fly anywhere."

"I gather from that you're not big on camping trips, either?"

"I have nothing against camping out. I would just need several pack mules to help me carry everything I'd want to take along," she said with a smile.

Gene burst out laughing.

Lori glanced around, trying to orient herself. "I never asked you before, but I'm assuming that your brother's okay with my staying at his place?"

"Preston's in Quantico right now taking a special training course, so I haven't been able to get hold of him," Gene said. "But don't worry, he won't care." Actually, Preston would probably try to take a piece of his hide when he found out, but what was life without a little excitement?

Silence settled between them as they left the main thoroughfare and entered a residential neighborhood.

"I just can't figure you out, Gene," Lori said at last. "You barely know me. Why are you so willing to help me?"

"I can't abide bullies and I'd like to equalize the odds against you."

His words were calm, but there was an undercurrent of a much darker emotion. "You sound like someone who knows what it's like to get picked on. Yet I can't imagine anyone in their right mind trying to give a man your size a hard time," she said, shifting to face him.

"I was a bit of a runt, one with health issues, until I turned sixteen and started to put on some muscle and weight," he said, meeting her gaze for a second, then looking away.

In those steady black eyes Lori caught a glimpse of shadows, the kind that grew in pain and hid in secrets. "You've had a rough life, haven't you?"

When he didn't answer right away, she spoke again. "We're going to be spending time together and I'd like to know more about you. We can't be friends and remain strangers. Things just don't work that way."

"You're right," he said with a nod. After several long moments, he spoke, his words measured and slow. "My life wasn't always hard, but things changed in a hurry after I turned ten. For a long time I was just another angry kid in the foster care system. I fought a lot—or maybe I should say I got beat up a lot," he added with a grim smile. "Eventually, Dan and I ended up at the same foster home. He and I joined forces there and watched each other's backs."

"How long were you there?"

"About six months. Then *Hosteen* Silver fostered us and took us to Copper Canyon. Everything changed for us after that." He paused, then added, "*Hosteen* Silver was a remarkable man."

"Will you tell me more about him?" she asked.

"Someday," he said, as he glanced into the rearview mirror.

"Are we being followed?" she asked, her stomach muscles tightening.

"No, it's still clear back there, but I better stay alert for trouble now. I have to make sure no one follows us to Preston's place."

He took a sharp right, then a left, always searching, but no threat appeared. Fifteen minutes later, they arrived at an upscale apartment complex. "They're all duplexes or townhomes?" she asked.

"Mostly. Preston pays a small fortune in rent, but he's not interested in buying a house, no matter how much business sense it makes. He doesn't like attachments of any kind. His apartment only has the basics." He paused, then grinned. "On the plus side, there's always plenty of beer in the fridge and he's got a real comfortable couch in front of a huge flat-screen TV. That's all my brother needs to be happy."

"No girlfriends?" she asked. "The few cops I've known over the years were very outgoing people with lots of friends."

"Preston's different," he said. "He's not big on talking, particularly about himself, so for all I know he's got a harem. I doubt it, though. He lives for his job."

"That doesn't sound like much of a life."

He shrugged. "It suits him. Preston values order and harmony. He sees his job as restoring the balance. One Navajo doesn't speak for another, but I think he was made for police work."

As they walked up to the door, she noticed the well-maintained landscaping and the individual parking slots that matched the apartment numbers. She'd never lived in a fancy place like this one. It was definitely a huge step up from her neighborhood.

As Gene flicked on the light switch and they went inside, she noticed that the place lacked a homey feel. The living room furnishings were just as Gene had described, a comfortable couch and a TV. Across the room, an overly long honey-brown baseball bat was propped on a special stand.

Following her gaze Gene laughed. "It looks like

a war club, doesn't it? That's my brother's baby—a 1920 Marathon. You should have seen him when he won the auction on eBay. You would have thought he'd scored the Hope Diamond."

"He's a baseball fan?"

"Not just a fan, a *rabid* fan," Gene said. "He sometimes flies to Phoenix to catch a 'Backs game."

She followed Gene into the dining area next to the kitchen. A breakfast bar served as a divider between the two spaces.

Gene opened the fridge and showed her what was inside. "If you get hungry, there are lots of cold cuts in here, some apples in the bottom drawer and a six-pack of cold beer."

"Thanks." She looked around again. "You mentioned sleeping on the couch, but I think you're taller than it is long."

"Yeah, but it folds out into a twin-size bed, or so I've been told. I've never tried it."

"And the bedrooms?"

"There are two down the hall. The one on the left is Preston's office. His bedroom's on the right and the bed has a memory foam mattress you're going to love. After spending a few nights on it, I've decided to get one for myself."

He helped carry her suitcase to Preston's bedroom and set it at the foot of the bed. "When you need to move it to the floor let me know. I'll get it out of your way."

"I really appreciate what you're doing," she said.

"I know I've turned your life, and whatever plans you had for your time in Hartley, upside down."

"You've helped me, too," he said.

She looked at him in surprise. "How? By helping you test your truck's braking system?"

He laughed, then shook his head. "I've had a tough time of it lately. Coping with all the details surrounding a loved one's death can be overwhelming. You've been a welcome, and beautiful, distraction."

As Lori looked into his dark eyes her heart began beating overtime. For those precious seconds, time stood still. She was aware of the warmth of his body and the spark of desire in his steady gaze.

"You're a mass of contradictions in one lovely package, Lori Baker," he whispered, tilting her chin upward and lowering his mouth to hers.

She felt the warmth of his breath on her lips and, with a sigh, closed her eyes. Suddenly the theme from *Dragnet* began to play loudly between them.

She jumped back. "What the—"

"It's my brother Preston's ring tone. That son of a gun sure has bad timing," he growled. He reached for his cell, but dropped it onto the carpet as he tried to press the send button.

Gene bent down, retrieved it and growled a one-word response. "What?"

His only answer was a dial tone.

Gene looked at Lori. "He hung up, would you believe it? He shows remarkable patience when it comes to police work, but with family, forget it." He chuckled and shook his head.

The mood broken, she went to open her suitcase. Though she always carried her laptop to work in her tote, for now, it would remain safely stored between folds in her clothing. "I've got to be at the office by seven forty-five tomorrow. Will you be able to give me a ride there? If it's too early for you, I can call a cab."

"That's not early. Ranchers are at work by dawn."

"Okay, then."

"You haven't had dinner yet. How's a pizza sound? I can have one delivered."

"Perfect, and it's on me."

An hour later they sat on the stools at the breakfast bar finishing the last few slices of a thick-crust combo. She'd eaten too much, but she hadn't had so much fun in a long time.

"Under different circumstances I would have called this a perfect date," she said.

"Me, too," he said, then wiped a bit of tomato sauce from the corner of her mouth with his napkin.

She stayed still, then finally drew a breath as he moved back.

"All done," he said.

"Thanks—for everything."

He held her gaze. "I know Harrington's always there at the back of your mind, but you need to remember one thing. You've come out ahead every time he's made a move."

"That's 'cause of the company I keep."

"We're more than even. After all, I got an exceptionally good pizza tonight," he said.

She laughed. "You know what would make this the best dinner ever? I know a place near here that has fantastic ice cream."

"You're talking about Ice Cold Heaven?"

"Yeah, you've been there?" she asked, and saw him nod. "It's my once-a-month special treat. I have to jog the next day to work the calories off, but it's sure worth it," Lori added.

"Then let's go. Maybe the sugar rush will help us figure out how we can set up the guy hounding you."

They left Preston's place, and as Gene locked the door, Lori headed to the pickup. She was looking around, enjoying the brightness of the moon and the pleasant breeze, when Gene suddenly yelled.

"Lori, look out!"

A man jumped out from the deep shadows beside the pickup, shoved her down to the pavement and grabbed her purse.

As he raced off, Gene instantly ran after him. The purse snatcher fled down the sidewalk, parallel to a pyracantha hedge on the roadside of the walk. He was fast, but Gene gained ground quickly. Halfway down the block, the man suddenly stopped, forcing his way through a gap in the hedge.

Gene heard a yelp, then a curse, and saw the man tugging at something. Gene focused, peering into the semidarkness, and saw that Lori's purse had caught in the shrubbery.

As the purse snatcher saw Gene almost upon him, he gave up trying to free Lori's bag and ran across the street. Soon he was heading down the narrow right-of-way behind the community center.

Gene knew he'd never make it through that gap in the hedge. He was too tall and too broad at the shoulders. Unable to jump over, he raced to the next opening, which turned out to be an adjacent driveway.

By the time Gene crossed the street and entered the narrow alley, the man was gone.

Gene looked around and spotted a big gathering of people enjoying a barbecue dinner at the rear patio of the complex's community center. "Where did he go?" Gene called out.

Several people looked over, but except for a few shrugs, he got no reaction whatsoever. After about ten seconds, a boy about seven pointed toward the corner of the building. "The man ran that way."

Gene walked a bit farther, visually sweeping the area in search of the purse snatcher, but all he could see was a parking lot full of cars and pickups. Muttering curses under his breath, he jogged back.

Lori was on the far side of the tall hedge and he could see only the top of her head. As he ran around to join her, he saw that she was on her knees, looking inside the foliage, her purse next to her on the sidewalk.

"He got the straps hooked on the brush and it snapped open," she said as he came up. "There's stuff all over the ground and among the leaves and thorns. Help me look around and make sure I'm not leaving anything behind."

One of the items still in her purse was a small penlight. She used it now to search, but her hand was shaking so badly it was hard to follow the beam.

"Here, let me hold it," Gene said. Taking it from her hands and working together, they retrieved her lipstick, wallet, keys, sunglasses and a handful of small items.

Once finished, Gene handed the penlight back to her, but her hand was trembling so hard she nearly dropped it.

"Lori, this isn't connected," Gene said softly. "A purse snatcher is probably working the area. We weren't followed here. I'd be willing to bet my last dollar on that," he said, placing his arm around her shoulders.

"You're wrong, Gene. It was him."

"Did you get a look at his face?" he pressed in a firm voice.

"No, it was too dark and he had on that stocking cap."

"You're upset, but you can't afford to make assumptions like that if for no other reason than you'll drive yourself crazy. Why don't you call the police and report the incident while I drive us over to get some ice cream? The change in scenery and a little comfort food can do wonders. Besides, standing around wringing our hands isn't going to do either of us any good."

As she dialed, Gene could see that she still wasn't convinced. "Lori, the man who has been coming after you isn't interested in just your purse."

"Yeah, that's a good point. I guess you're right. This must have been a separate incident," she said, though her tone suggested she thought otherwise.

They arrived about ten minutes later at Ice Cold Heaven. The ice-cream parlor, with the cloud-motif ceiling and ice-cream-cone-wielding cherubs painted on the walls, was a town favorite because of its home-style ice-cream cones and their unique flavors.

They picked up their order at the front, then sat at one of the two chair tables in a corner of the room. Lori ate her serving of "intense chocolate blast" slowly, savoring each mouthful. "For the sake of argument, let's say I'm right and that *was* Bud tonight. The purse thing could have been just another way of unnerving me. He could have found out who your brothers are, taken his chances and driven over to Preston's."

"Preston's address isn't listed anywhere public. Police officers are very careful about things like that."

"Maybe Bud has connections. Police officers can run a plate. P.I.'s also find ways to do the same thing. I can get that type of information at the DMV, too. Of course it's unethical to look into noncustomer records, and if I got caught I'd be out of a job."

"That brings up a whole new set of possibilities. I want you to think hard. Is there anyone working at the DMV who might dislike you enough to come after you like this?"

"No way. We're too busy to pay much attention to each other."

"There are always personality conflicts," he insisted.

"Sure, but you're talking *hate,* not just a personality issue. We don't spend enough time with each other, at least at work, for something like that to develop. We're always busy dealing with the public. Sure, I've had disagreements with the others there on occasion, but it's almost always work related and never lasts more than a day."

He looked around, then lowered his voice so only she could hear. "You're still afraid that Bud was the one who tried to grab your purse, so let's reason this out. When I first met you, a man was following you from a restaurant. He took off when I came on the scene, risking life and limb to get away. Then he tried to get into your house when he thought I was leaving. He should have waited but jumped the gun. That indicates just how eager he was to get inside while you were distracted, then catch you alone. That's not at all the way a purse snatcher works."

"You're right. The guy after me is a lot scarier, isn't he? I remember when I spotted him outside the restaurant, before you and I were supposed to meet for lunch," she said in a whisper-thin voice. "Maybe he wanted me to see him. So far, at least, part of his strategy has been to keep me on edge, running from shadows."

"A purse snatcher, on the other hand, wants something specific, strikes fast and then is gone. His work is dependent on opportunity and speed, nothing more."

"There's another way of looking at this," she said slowly. "Taking my purse could be just one more way of getting in my head. I have all my credit and debit cards there, my keys, my wallet, all the things that are part of my identity."

She took a breath and continued. "If Bud's goal had been to hurt me physically, he would have come at me differently from day one," she said. "All things considered, I think Harrington's playing with me, trying to make me sorry I ever turned him down. Or maybe he's just hoping to goad me into doing something stupid, so he can get me thrown in jail," she said, running an exasperated hand through her hair. "The problem is that I don't know how far he's going to take this sick game."

"Whatever the case, this guy's taking a lot of stupid chances, which tells me he's *not* a professional criminal."

"Maybe not, but he's making me crazy."

"Let's set all this aside for now. Maybe the answers will come to us tomorrow morning after we've had some sleep," he said, wishing he could say something that would make Lori smile again.

As they walked back to his pickup she looked over at him. "Let me be the one who sleeps on the love seat tonight. I'm smaller. I'll be more comfortable even if it does fold out into a bed."

"I'll be fine—but I'll be even better if you invite me to share the bed with you."

She gave him a slow, sexy smile that made his blood turn into a river of fire.

"Neither of us would get any sleep, then," she said, standing beside his truck.

He put his arms around her and pulled her close, letting her feel the heat from his body. He'd had many one-nighters, but the unrelenting need pounding through him now took him by surprise. He would have gladly traded ten years of his life for a night of slow, mind-blowing sex with her. "Losing a little sleep—would that be so bad?"

"Bad? No, I wouldn't say that. I'd probably love it," she said. "Then, afterward, I'd be filled with regret because I'm not ready for that. To me, lovemaking should be just that—two people who care so deeply for each other that everything in them demands they become one. It's about having two hearts with one steady beat."

"It doesn't always have to be that way. I can make you feel things that will rock you to the core again and again," he said, his voice low, his body hard with desire.

She took a shaky breath and he felt her wavering. Her gaze drifted down to the center of his jeans and she licked her lips nervously. Just watching her made his body tighten to such an impossible level he thought he'd explode. "I'll make it good," he murmured.

She swallowed several times. "You want me, and maybe I want you, too, but in here," she said, pointing to her heart, "I need more than heat. I want to feel a yearning so intense that a union is the only way for me to find peace."

It took everything he had not to try and get her to change her mind. He knew he could pull her into his arms and kiss her senseless. He knew how to make a woman melt in his arms. Yet what she really wanted wasn't something he could give her.

"Your choice, darling." He brushed his knuckles on her cheek and heard her fractured sigh. "I'll sleep in the living room and dream of you."

Chapter Eight

As they reached Preston's place, Lori saw a woman in her mid-fifties come out from one of the adjoining town houses. She hurried toward them, waving her arms.

The slender woman, with flaming red hair, greeted them as they got out of the car. Her large Labrador-mix dog remained standing by her town house's open doorway, snarling and barking with excitement.

"Someone tried to break into Preston's place just a few minutes ago," she told Gene. "I ran him off by threatening to let Bitsy have a go at him," she added, pointing to the large mass of black fur. The dog's white teeth flashed in the light and drool dripped from its jowls.

"No wonder he ran," Lori said.

The woman smiled. "Most of the time she's the sweetest dog in the world, but when Bitsy senses a threat and gets riled up she's a holy terror," she said. "The two of us were coming back from our evening walk when Bitsy saw the guy lurking around the back window. He was wearing a dark shirt, a sweat-shirt, I think, and a baseball cap pulled down low on his forehead. He had something sharp, maybe a knife or chisel, for prying open a window," she said. "Bitsy went nuts and wanted to take a chunk out of him. The guy heard her growling and took off quick as lightning between the buildings." She pointed. "That's the last I saw of him, but the police are on their way."

Just as she finished speaking, two patrol cars with flashing red lights turned into the complex and drove up.

Two officers stepped out of the units and walked toward them. "Who's Patty McDermott?" the taller of the two asked.

"I am, and the guy ran that way," Patty said, pointing. "I figured you'd want to know since one of your officers, Detective Bowman, lives at the apartment he was planning to break into."

"Dispatch said you thought the man had a weapon, maybe a knife? Did he threaten you?" the second officer asked.

Patty shook her head. "No. Bitsy and I startled him and he ran. I guess he didn't want the kind of trouble my dog could give him. As for the weapon… I'm thinking now it may have been a chisel. Whatever it was, I know it had a yellow handle."

The officer turned to look at the dog, who was still growling. "Ma'am, maybe you should close that door," he said.

"She won't move without a specific command—or if she thinks I'm being threatened—but if it'll make you feel better…"

"It would," the officer said instantly.

As Patty moved away, the other cop, whose name tag identified him as Officer Murray, turned to Gene. "You're one of Preston's brothers, right? The rancher?"

"Yeah," Gene said with a half smile, then filled him in.

The officer took some notes, then glanced at Lori. "You should have done as Sergeant Chavez recommended, ma'am. Leaving town, at least until we can identify a suspect, is still your best course of action."

"Like you, Officer, I have a job and responsibilities here," she said in a harsher voice than she'd intended. Having to defend her reasons for staying annoyed her. She wasn't the criminal; she was the victim.

As soon as the thought formed, she cringed. To become a bona fide victim, all she'd have to do was start thinking of herself as one. "I'm not the problem here, Officer. The man after me is. That's who you need to concentrate on."

"How sure are you that Detective Bowman wasn't the intended target? After all, this is *his* place," the officer said, glancing at Gene then Lori.

"Preston's in Quantico right now," Gene said, "so his parking space is empty. Anyone seriously looking for him would have known he wasn't here. I suppose it might have been a burglar randomly targeting apartments where nobody's home. But considering that there was also an attempted purse snatching earlier where Ms. Baker was the target, I think we're pushing the bounds of coincidence."

"It's not that unlikely. With the police slowdown, there's been a rise in property crimes. They know we can't be everywhere," the officer said.

"So what now?" she said.

"We'll do what we can, including checking around the window surfaces, but if the guy didn't leave usable prints, there won't be much we can do. We'll ask around and see if anyone else saw the man in the cap and windbreaker."

As the officer went to join the other patrolman, who was coming around from the back of the building, Lori looked over at Gene. "When they think one of their own is threatened in any way, they can sure move fast."

"Theirs is a special brotherhood. They've got each other's backs. They have to. Cops can make some bad enemies," he said. "But if you're thinking that they got here double time for one of their own but not for you, you're not taking one important fact into account. Their suspect was still here when Patty called."

"And maybe still is?" Lori's eyes widened and she looked around.

"Let's go inside," Gene said with a nod and hurried with her into Preston's home.

Lori sat on the sofa while Gene stood next to the window, peering outside.

About fifteen minutes later, they heard a knock at the door. Gene let Officer Murray in. "We've spoken to some of the residents," Officer Murray said. "Two people claimed to have seen a dark-colored van driving away. The driver was wearing a baseball cap."

"The man who's been after Ms. Baker drives a dark van," Gene said. "Anyone see a plate?"

He shook his head. "Only that he had a yellow, old, basic state tag. We'll try to have patrols drive through this area more often, but we've done all we can at this point."

As soon as the officer left, Lori picked up her purse. "I want to go by Bud's home and check to see if those plates are still on his truck."

"All right. Let's go take a look."

As Gene drove out of the complex, Lori thought of how things might have turned out if Gene hadn't been driving down that street the other day.

She glanced at him and, seeing the way his big, strong hands gripped the wheel, she swallowed back a sigh. Her gaze drifted over his strong shoulder, then downward. The bulge she'd seen in his jeans when he'd tried to talk her into a night of steamy sex also told her he was extremely well endowed.

If truth be told, she'd never been more tempted to have a wild night of sex in her life.

"What's on your mind?" he asked, a smile hovering at the corners of his mouth.

She drew in her breath, and didn't look directly at him, wondering if her expression had somehow given her away. "I was just trying to understand you," she said.

"Uh-uh. That wasn't it."

"Oh, be quiet," she said.

A short while later they entered Harrington's neighborhood. Gene slowed down to a crawl as he drove past Harrington's house.

"The plates aren't on the truck!" she said quickly. "You know that he'll put them back on, so let's stick around. He's bound to show up."

"At least we know that he's been here since I last drove by. Either that, or someone stole his mail," Gene said, pointing.

"But his newspapers are still on the porch," she pointed out.

"Maybe he needed his mail for business reasons but didn't want to bother with the rest. I have a feeling that he's found somewhere else to stay, so he might not come back again for days. Even if we sat here all night, our only guarantee is that you're going to be real sleepy at work tomorrow."

She let her breath out in a whoosh. "Yeah, you're right, and since he already knows your vehicle, he'll steer clear if he spots us before we do him," she said. "Our problem is that he also knows where Preston lives—that is, if we assume *he* was the one there tonight."

"I'm not ready to conclude that," he said, "but something still feels off to me. That includes the fact that it doesn't really look like he's currently living here." After a long silence, he continued. "We agree on one thing, though. Going back to Preston's tonight is too risky. We need a new place."

"I don't know where else to go," she said. "I'm a walking target."

"Let me drop my truck off at my brother Paul's place. When he flies out, he always takes a cab to the airport, so he won't mind us borrowing his Jeep. Then we'll go to the one place I know your stalker will have a very hard time finding."

"Where's that?"

"My foster father's home in Copper Canyon. Even the locals have trouble finding the place without a map. At night, with no lights for miles, it's pitch-black around there. Unless you know the terrain by heart, it's impossible to drive around after sundown without risking your tires, getting stuck or driving into an arroyo. The best thing is that the animals in the area will always let you know when there's an intruder."

"You mean like lots of barking dogs?"

"No, more like cougars, coyotes, mule deer and the flocks of birds that live all throughout Copper Canyon," he said. "The address won't be listed anywhere, either, because there's no address to speak of. There's no delivery service, either, only a rural post office miles away."

"Just how far away is this place?"

"It's an hour's drive there and back, but I can make sure you get to work on time and I can pick you up at the end of your shift. That'll give Sergeant Chavez more time to come up with some answers. I'll also look into things myself while you're at work, safe and sound."

"We're only open half a day on Saturday, so you'd have to pick me up just after noon, not five-thirty. Are you sure about all this?"

"Yes, I don't mind the back and forth, but the final decision is yours," Gene said. "I know you'd probably be more comfortable staying in town, but as you said, we're running out of options."

"Living in town has always been a necessity for me. That's where the jobs are."

"Are you telling me that you're a country girl at heart?"

"I might be, I don't know. I've never had the chance to find out. All I can say is that I like open spaces and I love being around animals. I've often pictured what it would be like to live on a big ranch, but those are just fantasies."

He said nothing for several minutes. "Do you do that often?"

"What?"

"Fantasize," he said.

"More than I should."

He gave her one of his slow, killer grins, his eyes on hers. That look drew her in and a dozen heart-stopping, deliciously tempting images popped into her head.

She looked away quickly, but not before seeing the even wider grin on his face.

They soon arrived at a popular coffee shop not far from the community college and Gene parked in the back near a blue Jeep.

"Your brother must really love coffee," she said, glancing around and wondering where, exactly, Paul lived.

"Yeah, he does, but that's not why he lives here. He's friends with the owner of the coffee shop, and is getting the upstairs apartment rent-free in exchange for security services. Paul has cameras mounted everywhere, along with sophisticated monitoring systems. That's why he leaves the Jeep here instead of at the airport, and why I knew my truck would be safe, too."

They placed her things in Paul's Jeep, then set off again almost right away, making their way out of Hartley.

"I can't see anything beyond the headlights, can you?" After leaving town they'd entered a no-man's-land between little farm communities that were nothing more than small clusters of buildings beside the highway.

"There's not much to see along this stretch, except

dry grassland. That'll change before too long. I know the route by heart, so all I have to worry about is some large animal, like a cow, straying out onto the road."

The hypnotic effect of the white line on the highway and the low rumble of the knobby tires made her sleepy. Although she hadn't meant to, Lori dozed off sometime after midnight. It wasn't until they hit a bad bump that she woke up with a start.

"Wow, I fell asleep? I'm sorry! I should have been talking and helping you stay awake."

"You needed the rest," he said. "Don't worry about it. Right now this dirt road is so rough there's no way I'm going to drift off."

"Yeah, but before, with miles of nothing and more nothing, you could have fallen asleep behind the wheel," she said, shaking the cobwebs out of her mind. "I'm sorry I let you down like that."

"You didn't. This route is special to me. What you described as miles of nothing, I see as the road to and from home. Up ahead is the canyon where Dan and I used to teach our younger brothers hiking skills. Then there's the narrow, steep cliff beyond there. None of us could ever climb up to the top without help. The only person who could was *Hosteen* Silver. He could find handholds where all we saw was naked sandstone."

"I didn't mean to sound flip," she said, apologizing quickly. "It's just that, to me, particularly in the dark, it just seems so empty here."

"You can always talk straight with me. No offense taken," he said. "I know what it's like to look at this place through the eyes of a stranger. I remember the first time I came here. It was at night, like now, when the darkness pretty much swallowed up everything in its path. I felt as if I'd fallen into a hole and I was scared to death I'd never be able to crawl back out. Everything was quiet, and scary."

"You were a city kid?"

"I grew up in Albuquerque," he said, nodding. "To me, the Rez was just someplace 'out there.' When I said that *Hosteen* Silver found Dan and me and gave us a new life, I meant every word of it. At first the Rez was like another planet to us—a wilderness. The first few months, we were equal parts scared and exhausted. *Hosteen* Silver demanded a lot from us, and the fact that he was a *hataalii,* a medicine man, had us both spooked. We had no idea what to expect."

"Did you have to attend ceremonies and things like that?" she asked.

"No, he never pushed his beliefs on us. He'd explain Navajo ways, and then let us choose for ourselves whether we wanted to accept them or not. All he demanded was that we show the proper respect," Gene said. "In time we came to understand that the Navajo way was part of us, just like it was of him." He paused, then continued. "The most important lesson *Hosteen* Silver taught us is that everyone and everything is connected. Life, taken as a whole, forms a pattern, and a man can only walk in beauty if he finds his place within that."

Lori watched Gene closely as he spoke. There was a calm self-assurance about him that drew her. He'd seen the worst and best of life, and somewhere along the way had found himself. "You're not like anyone I've ever met."

He laughed. "I'm not that different from any other man. I just know what I want and what I need and, unlike some, I know the difference between the two."

"You found a new identity in this canyon and, after that, charted your own course. That planning and effort paid off for you, but I've always been wary of making too many plans. They can hem you in."

"Plans shouldn't be set in stone. For me, they're more like a road map to help me get where I'm going," he said.

"Where's that?"

"A secure life—one earned from tending to animals and the land. Both will take care of a man as long as a man takes care of them. That's all part of the pattern, and respecting it brings harmony."

"You've said that *Hosteen* Silver was a remarkable man, but you're pretty amazing yourself."

He shook his head. "No, I'm just an ordinary guy who has a way with animals, and needs to work outside in the fresh air to be happy."

"Are you good with all animals, or just horses?"

"I'm particularly good with horses, but it doesn't stop there. I can read animals. It's as if a part of me becomes a part of them and that allows us to communicate." He paused. "It may sound a little crazy, but it's true."

"No, it doesn't sound crazy. I think it's amazing."

"Whenever I'm close to an animal, I can read its moods. I know if it's afraid, or if it's just being stubborn," he said, then told her about Grit. "He had Paul pinned to the rails, but Grit was just testing him."

She laughed, hearing about Paul's encounter with the horse. "Your ranch, your life sounds just about perfect—horses to ride and train, and a place where you can breathe free and follow your own rules."

"It's that sense of freedom that called me, and I never doubted I could make it work." He slowed, turned a sharp left and drove up a dirt road. "What about you? Where's your heart leading you?"

She suppressed a sigh. "My father once accused me of just coasting through life, but that's not true. To find what's right for me I may have to travel a lot of empty roads. So I live one day at a time. You never know what's just around the bend."

"By leaving yourself open to all possibilities, you become more vulnerable than you realize. That's a lesson I learned in foster care," he said. "The younger kids would come into the system filled with hope that maybe they'd go back to their parents before long, or that they'd find new adoptive

ones who'd love them. They saw every day as a chance waiting to unfold. Slowly, days would turn into years, and hopes into cynicism or anger."

"I don't see what I'm doing as an exercise in hope. To me, it's about finding my destiny."

"You're an unusual woman," he said softly.

"Thank you. I mean, was that a compliment?"

"Yes, it was," he answered, laughing. "In your own way, you're a romantic."

"Sure I am, but that doesn't mean I'm looking for perfection—just the right fit."

"That sometimes means the coming together of opposites. Navajo teachings say that everything has two sides. Light needs dark, just as good needs evil to balance each other. A man also needs a woman, and a woman, a man. By pairing they become whole."

His words drifted over her like an intimate caress that left her tingling. She drew in a shaky breath. Gene brought an intensity, a sparkle of something she'd yet to define, to every moment. Just being with him made her feel more alive, more vibrant.

At last they arrived at a one-lane wooden bridge across a deep arroyo. Gene slowed to a crawl and they proceeded across, the tires rumbling on the rough timbers below. Ahead, Lori could just about make out the sandstone walls of a high bluff.

Gene came to a stop and switched off the headlights, leaving only his dim parking lights on. He then put the Jeep in low gear, and headed toward a

dark area of the bluff. As they drew near, Lori saw that the dirt road they were taking would lead them through a narrow pass flanked by two high cliffs.

"We're now entering Copper Canyon," he said.

As they drove between the walls, barely a hundred yards apart, she saw the canyon open up ahead. It widened to the point she could no longer see any details, just dark, high cliffs on both sides. The arroyo lay to their left now.

"It's beautiful and mysterious," she said. "But it's so isolated. You must have felt lonely out here."

"I know it seems like a big empty box at first, but it's filled with life. Look ahead," he said, pointing as he came to a stop.

She leaned forward and drew in a sharp breath. "What is that? A feral dog?"

"No, a coyote. There are a lot of them out here."

She waited for him to keep driving, but they remained where they were. "The house is farther up?" she asked, and saw him nod. After several minutes she added, "Shouldn't we keep going?"

"I want to watch for a bit. If anything's out of place, that coyote will let me know."

She watched the animal watching them, its eyes gleaming in the low glow of the parking lights. Eventually it trotted off.

Lori spotted movement in a nearby shrub. As she focused on it, a small creature, maybe a rat, came out of hiding. It turned around and began sniffing the ground, but before it could go far, a big bird swooped down, wings outstretched, and grabbed the animal in its talons. In a flash, it disappeared into the night.

"The owl has taken a late supper," he said. After a long while, he placed the Jeep in gear again. "Everything is as it should be out here. Let's go on."

"I hope someday I can see your ranch, too," she said, straining to catch a clear glimpse of what lay ahead.

"Would you really like that?"

"Very much so," she said.

His dark eyes focused intently on her. The power of that one look nearly took her breath away. It reminded her of the old saying, "still waters run deep." The real measure of the man by her side lay well beyond what he allowed the world to see.

"Someday I'll take you there and show you around. Life has a different rhythm at Two Springs Ranch."

The road circled left, eventually reaching a low spot in the arroyo. As they dropped down inside, the Jeep fishtailed slightly in the sand. Soon they rose out of the depression onto more solid ground. A hundred yards ahead, across a small meadow, was a rectangular stucco frame house nestled near the opposite wall of the canyon. Moonlight shined down on its metal roof, giving it a soft, almost unearthly glow.

Gene parked close to the front door. "Come on.

Let's get inside," he said, then reached for her suitcase while she picked up her large tote.

"The moonlight makes the house look enchanted, magical," she said, as they walked to the raised front porch. "Somehow it fits you."

He shook his head. "I have no magic. That was solely *Hosteen* Silver's thing." He searched his pocket for the key to the dead bolt. "He could do things that defied logic at times."

"Like what?"

"He'd often know things before they happened. At first I thought that he studied people, then predicted their behavior, but there was more to it than that."

He flicked on the light switch. "No one lives here now, but that'll change when Kyle, one of my brothers who's serving with NCIS overseas, comes home to stay."

"Where does the electricity come from? Is there a generator, and batteries?"

"No, there's a buried power line that runs out the back and to the highway along a very narrow footpath between the cliffs. It's not wide enough for vehicles, though, and not too many people know about it."

She smiled. "Now it sounds even more like a magical place—with a secret path to the road and all.

"There's a real sense of peace here," she added softly. "Maybe it's the furnishings, or the beautiful Navajo blankets that are draped over the couch and hang on the wall. I don't know why, really, but I feel...at home."

"People often say that," he told her. "When Dan and I lived here with *Hosteen* Silver, friends were always dropping by. Patients, too, but they generally went to the six-sided log medicine hogan out in the back. It's hidden by the house when you come in by road."

"All my Navajo friends in high school grew up in town and none of them had a hogan. You've certainly led an interesting life," she said. "I'd love to hear more about your time here in Copper Canyon."

"Maybe tomorrow," he said. "It's past one in the morning and you'll have to get up early to get to work on time. When, exactly, do you have to be there in the morning?"

"We don't take lunch because we close at noon, so if I don't take a break, I don't have to come in till nine-fifteen."

"Okay, then. Let's go make up one of the beds and we'll talk as we work."

He led her down the short central hall and into the first bedroom on his left. There were two twin beds inside. "I think you'll find these beds comfortable. The mattresses are foam now, but originally they were filled with straw and wool from our sheep."

"You had sheep?"

"*Hosteen* had a small flock, and we and the guys who came after us tended them. He used to say that the sheep and the land provided for us and that's why we'd never go hungry."

"Did that ever happen to you?" she asked softly. "Go hungry, I mean."

He nodded slowly. "My mom and dad were alcoholics. Buying booze was their priority, so often there was nothing in the fridge. When I couldn't beg food from the neighbors I'd go to bed early, because once I fell asleep my empty stomach wouldn't bother me so much."

The reality of what his life had been like at one time stunned her. She reached for his hand and covered it with hers. She wanted to say something deep, or something wise that would make it all better, but couldn't find the right words.

"I'm sorry you had to go through that," she found herself saying, meaning every word, and wishing it didn't sound so lame.

"Everything has two sides, remember?" he said. "Those days taught me to appreciate the good times."

As she looked at Gene, she saw a man whose courage had been forged by adversity. After seeing the darkest spot in hell, nothing much could frighten him.

"You're all set now," Gene said, as he finished tucking in the sheet. "I'll start a fire in the fireplace. The house will stay warm till morning, then." Seeing her yawn, he smiled. "Get some rest. One good thing about Copper Canyon is how quickly sleep comes to everyone out here."

"I didn't bring an alarm clock. Do you have one?" she asked as he started to leave.

"No, but it's not necessary. I always wake up before daybreak. It's an old habit. It doesn't matter what time I go to bed."

"Will you wake me up?"

"Before daybreak?"

"Yeah. I'd like to look around and see Copper Canyon by daylight," she said.

"Okay. I'll give you a tour first thing tomorrow morning. There's a lot to see. It's a completely different place when the sun's out."

"And, Gene?"

He turned his head as he reached the doorway.

"Thanks for sticking with me."

Electricity charged the air between them as he met her gaze and held it. She didn't want him to leave—and he didn't want to go.

"I won't be far. If you need me, call," he said in a rough voice, and closed the door.

She needed him—in every possible way. Yet that was one line she didn't dare cross. If she did, instinct told her she might never find her way back again.

Chapter Nine

Gene felt the blood thundering through him. The idea of Lori lying in his old bed just out of his reach was making him crazy inside. She was all softness and gentle curves, a woman practically made to be loved. His body hardened thinking about her.

Though it defied logic, since he scarcely knew her, the crazy attraction between them was real. Lori had touched him in a way he couldn't—or maybe didn't want—to fight. He loved her smiles, her spirit, and just being near her was a constant reminder that he was a man, and she, a woman.

Swearing softly, he got busy building a fire in the large cast-iron fireplace insert, a design *Hosteen* Silver had carefully selected because it would provide effective heat for hours.

Looking at the bright flames behind the glass and feeling the heat now flowing into the room, he remembered his foster father's teachings. A man and a woman needed each other to be complete. That, too, was part of the pattern.

After making sure he had a clear view of the front

door, Gene lay down on the couch. The stillness in the house and warmth of the fire made him drift quickly to sleep, but even there, her arms found him.

LORI OPENED HER EYES SLOWLY. The cool, crisp air filtering through the narrow opening in the window nudged her awake gently. As she sat up she heard a soft rustling in the leaves outside. Maybe it was a cottontail or quail searching for seeds.

The peaceful smile on her face disappeared in a flash as a deep, menacing growl sounded outside, somewhere close by. Cold with dread, she crept out of bed and across the room.

Afraid to see what was outside, she didn't watch where she was going and smashed her toe on the edge of her suitcase, still on the floor where she'd left it. Covering her mouth with one hand, she muffled a yelp and breathed in and out till the pain passed.

Lori inched over to the window and peered out. The first thing she saw was Gene, standing completely still. Then, following his gaze, Lori saw a huge black bear about ten feet from him.

She drew in a sharp breath and stared in horror as the bear slowly walked up to Gene and dropped what it had in its mouth like some giant retriever. It then growled again, a softer sound this time, but still terrifying.

To her surprise, Gene seemed calm. "The kill

is yours. Eat it in peace and live, my brother," she heard him say.

Lori remained rooted to the spot, watching. The bear calmly picked up the animal it had caught, holding it in its powerful jaws, but didn't move away.

Gene began to chant, his voice strong and compelling. Even though she didn't understand the words, she felt the power of the song. It rose into the air and danced through the pines, and as it did, everything stilled. It was as if nature itself was holding its breath, listening.

Man and bear continued to stand face-to-face, but neither seemed afraid. Then the massive animal turned around slowly and walked away.

Lori stumbled back from the window. Her hands were shaking and her body felt ice-cold. Shivers ran up her spine, but that had nothing to do with the breeze coming from the open window. While she struggled to even her heart rate, she heard a soft knock at her door.

"Time to get up," Gene said from the hall.

Without even thinking, Lori opened her door and launched herself into his arms.

"I heard the growl, went to the window and saw you and that bear! I'm so glad you're okay." She was trembling and couldn't make herself stop. "How did you keep from running?"

"That would have been a fatal mistake. *Prey* runs," he said, wrapping his arms tightly around her. "More importantly, I was never in any danger. On some level, I know you sensed that, too."

She nodded slowly. "What made *you* so sure he wouldn't attack? Your gift with animals?"

"Partly, yes, but in this case, that's not the whole story. Bear medicine, ritual items I carry in my medicine bag, link me to the animal and make him my spiritual brother. Neither one of us would harm the other. I also carry the fetish of a bear with me. It was a gift from *Hosteen* Silver. He chose it especially for me."

"Why a bear?" Lori's childhood friends had taught her about some of their tribal beliefs, and fetishes were common.

"*Hosteen* Silver saw me as a loner, despite my closeness to my brothers. He told me that Bear's power was made strong in solitude, and though Bear had a dark side, he also stood for confidence and inner stillness." He looked into her eyes. "I'm sorry you were scared, but you never have to be when I'm near."

As desire shimmered to life between them, he tilted her face upward. Gene took her mouth slowly, filling her senses with a sweet fire.

His arms tightened around her until she could feel his heart beating against hers. Lori sighed softly, and almost instantly, he deepened the kiss.

Following her heart, she surrendered to the sensations rippling through her. Nothing else mattered right now but him. As she melted against him, his kiss became hotter, wetter and more demanding.

The warmth inside her soon became a raging fire that started at the center of her being and spread outward. Lori clung to his shoulders, drinking in his taste, loving his roughness.

He broke the kiss with a groan and looked into her eyes. "In another minute I won't be able to stop, and you won't want me to. Decide now, Lori."

His body was pressed intimately against hers, and she knew he was ready. All she'd have to do was kiss him again. Yet fear held her back. Her feelings for him were so intense they were nearly overwhelming. In his arms, she'd turned into someone she scarcely recognized.

She took a step back. "I...can't." Unable to look into the fire that still burned in his eyes, she turned away and walked to her suitcase. It took her a moment to be able to say anything else, but hearing him start to leave, she glanced back at him with a shaky smile. "You promised to show me Copper Canyon this morning, remember?" she said. "Once you're sure the bear's long gone, maybe we can walk around?"

"Bear won't hurt you."

For a moment she was sure his words had more than one meaning. Looking away, she forced her tone to stay light. "The bear likes *you* but it might see me as an early lunch. I'm better tasting than that poor creature it was carrying."

He smiled slowly. "You're right about that, but Bear won't take what's not his."

Lori took an unsteady breath. "Let me put some shoes on," she said, tearing her gaze away. The way he was looking at her made it impossible for her to think.

"If you have boots, wear them. The sun's coming over the ridge right now, and snakes might be coming out to lie on the rocks to warm up."

"I have shooties—low boots," she said. "Give me a chance to wash up and I'll join you in a sec."

It took her longer than she'd said, but by the time she met him in the living room her pulse was beating at a normal rate again. "When I pictured myself living a rural life, I'd see dogs, horses, cattle and even sheep—but I never factored in the wild part of nature. Now that I've seen it up close, I'm absolutely certain that I can do without bears the size of tanks, and snakes," she said and smiled.

"Everything, including bears and snakes, are part of the pattern. The challenge is to find your place within that."

His confidence seemed so unshakable. An instinct she didn't quite understand assured her she would be safe with him no matter where they went.

They soon left the house, taking a trail that led upward from the canyon floor toward the steep mesa to the east.

"*Hosteen* Silver would take this same trail every morning," he said. "Then, as the sun rose, he'd

take a pinch of pollen from his medicine pouch and throw it up into the air as an offering to Dawn."

"Do you do that, too?" she asked.

"When I'm at the ranch, yes, but that doesn't make me a Traditionalist like he was. I'm what some call a Modernist. I respect the old ways and honor the beliefs of my people, the *Diné,* but not at the exclusion of modern conveniences or technology. Like most Navajos, I go to the doctor if I need to, but I don't necessarily exclude a *hataalii* from that picture."

"You walk between two cultures," she said with a nod.

He nodded. "There's balance in being a Modernist, too."

When they reached the cliff, she followed him up the steep trail. A colorful wall of sandstone rose to their right at a near vertical angle. The tilted layers of ancient sedimentary rock, weathered at different rates, provided a shelf of rock, a natural path up the canyon wall.

She concentrated on where she placed her feet, aware of the steep drop-off to her left, and wondered just how high they were going. The only times she'd risk a look down into the canyon was during breaks when they were standing still. Otherwise, it would make her feel disoriented.

She concentrated on the path before her until Gene stopped at a wide spot in the trail.

"Look around us," he said. "Have you ever seen

anything so beautiful? This is Copper Canyon at its best."

Illuminated by the early-morning sun, the canyon wall to the west was streaked in reds, oranges and earthy tans. Farther down, still in the shadow, those same walls became a palette of dark blues, purples and deep browns.

"And look up," he said.

As the sun continued to rise in the east, the trees above them seemed to glow in brilliant blue-greens.

"When I was a kid, if Wind was still, or blowing just right, we'd hear *Hosteen*'s prayer to the dawn drifting down the canyon. We'd make out the words *'Hozhone nas clee,'* now all is well, and, somehow, we knew it would be because he was part of this land and it was a part of him."

"This place is part of you, too," she said. "It taught you to be hardy and resilient, the same qualities that enable the desert to survive."

Gene nodded slowly. "All that's true, but *Hosteen* Silver gave me an even greater gift. He taught me that if I believe in myself, I'd never know failure, because I'd see each setback as just another stumbling block I'd need to overcome."

As he watched the desert below, she watched him. It was impossible not to be drawn to Gene, this man who was as strong as he was gentle. She remembered how it had felt to be pressed against his hard chest, and how she'd clung to his shoulders for the

strength to stand. Everything in her had yearned to give in.

Afraid that he'd somehow guess the turn her thoughts had taken, she leaned against the cold rock face, her feet spread out in front of her.

As she took a breath, she heard a dry shaking rattle. The distinctive sound reverberated with deadly intent. The only time she'd ever heard a rattlesnake had been on a nature show on TV, but listening to it up close was far, far worse. If death had a sound, that was it.

"Don't move," Gene said softly. "I see it." He pointed to a recess on a flat rock just behind her. "Its body has a bulge, and it's still sluggish from the cold. It caught something last night, probably a mouse, so it's not interested in you. It's looking for a warm spot to lie in while it digests its food. Take a slow step to your right. You'll free its path so it can move out into the sun."

As she edged away, Gene began chanting, the cadence and rhythm making it sound like a prayer and song all in one.

Though it took all her willpower not to just jump away, she inched aside until Gene held up one hand. The second he did, she stopped.

Gene stepped forward and forced Lori to hug the rock as he placed his body between her and the snake. She wanted to protect him by making him edge away, but any movement at all now would only enhance the danger to both of them.

The rattler, now silent, slithered up the path several feet, then moved out onto a flat boulder beneath an overhang now illuminated in sunshine.

"Everything's okay now, but you're still being watched," he said, "so don't move in that direction."

"I wouldn't dream of it," she said, starting back down the trail. "That beautiful chant—was it a prayer or a song?"

"Both. It's called a *Hozonji,* a good luck song, but the exact wording has to remain a secret between me and the powers I called upon for help. *Hozonjis* are passed down in families, and in my case, it was a gift from *Hosteen* Silver."

Noticing how quickly she was moving, he reached for her shoulder, slowing her down. "You don't have to hurry. The snake won't chase you."

"I know you're right, but I hate snakes. They're such sneaky creatures."

He shook his head. "Snakes will only strike a human if they feel threatened. They're neither good nor evil. They have a right to hunt for food, and they help man by keeping the rodent population down. They're part of the circle of life."

Lori shook her head. "In this, we'll have to agree to disagree. They're sneaks. At least a bear comes at you in the open, face on."

"That's because Bear has strength on its side. Snake uses stealth because it's the best weapon it has. As the earthly manifestation of the Lightning

People, Snake is said to have the power to bring rain to the desert. That's why they shouldn't be killed."

She said nothing for several long moments, then turned her head to look at him. "When you said you had a way with animals, I never dreamed that included bears and snakes."

"Everything's connected. Knowing that is how we maintain the *hózh*."

"I don't know what that means. Will you explain it to me?"

"It's living harmoniously and in perfect balance with everything that surrounds us," he said as they stepped onto the canyon floor. "It's seeing the pattern in the threads that connect all of life. The effects of even one careless act can be very far-reaching, like ripples in a pond."

She thought about what he'd said. "How does evil fit into the pattern?"

"Nothing is completely evil," he said. "Evil is just something that resists being brought under control. Once it's in check, it becomes part of the pattern again. Everything in life has two sides, and each is needed to balance the other."

"So by helping me, you're honoring the pattern because you're keeping evil in check?"

"Like that, yes."

"I'm glad we're friends." One thing was certain. No matter what happened, she'd never forget Gene.

Almost as if he'd guessed what she'd left unsaid, he brushed the side of her face with his palm.

"There's balance between us. You've brought something very special into my life."

When he didn't elaborate after a few seconds, she asked, "What special thing did I bring into your life?" She reached for his hand as they walked back to the house.

"Softness," he said, then brought her hand up and kissed it. "I'm sorry that you're in trouble, but I'm not sorry that you stepped into my life—though I wish it hadn't been in front of my truck."

She laughed. "I guess that's one instance where evil brought something good."

"Now the rest is up to us." Before she could answer, he gestured toward the house. "Get ready to go. We'll pick up breakfast along the way."

Lori glanced around her, then sighed softly. For some reason she didn't quite understand, the thought of leaving Copper Canyon saddened her. "I wish we didn't have to go. I like it here...with you."

"Yet when we're together you always pull away." He looked into her eyes, as if searching for an answer there. "What are you most afraid of—me, or you?"

Deep inside she knew the truth, but facing it now jolted her to the core. "I..." Seeing the slow simmering fire in Gene's eyes filled her with desire.

"The feelings between us are real. Listen to your heart."

"I don't doubt the feelings—I just don't trust

them. Love has a dark side. I learned that lesson as
a kid."

"I trust you—trust me," he said. "Tell me what
you're afraid of."

Lori swallowed hard. He'd repeatedly risked his
life for her, and just moments ago, he'd placed himself between her and harm.

"You're right. You deserve more from me than secrets." She took a deep breath, gathering her courage. This was something she'd never discussed with
anyone. She'd buried the past deep inside her, or
so she'd thought, but some things refused to stay
hidden.

"My mom and dad adored each other," she began
at last. "Everyone called them the perfect couple and
they were constantly being invited to parties. Then
one day, out of the blue, they came to tell me that
they were splitting up. I don't know what happened
between them, obviously it was something big, but
I saw love turn into hate practically in the blink of
an eye."

"It happens," he said, "but not knowing why made
that even tougher on you."

"That's true," she said, then after a beat continued. "Things went downhill fast from that point on,
too. After their divorce I became surplus goods, the
kid no one wanted. They each had new partners and
I was part of the old. More than anything I wanted
them to love each other again, but all I did was
come between them. I became the one thing they

could use to manipulate each other. What they did hurt me deeply, but more importantly, it changed me. I don't know if I'm still capable of trusting in love. To this day, I've never been able to give my heart to anyone without keeping a part of me safely out of reach."

"And you won't accept anything less than all from yourself, or another, for the same reason. You want a commitment that means something, above and beyond words," he said, understanding. "But the future is always shifting and changing. It's hard to get a bead on a moving target. Love requires a leap of faith."

"How about if we take things one tiny leap at a time, at least for now?" she asked with a tremulous smile.

"I can handle that."

His acceptance of her just as she was left her yearning to touch him, to assure herself that he was real. Gathering her courage, Lori stood on tiptoe and brought his mouth down to meet hers. Her kiss, intended to say thank-you, turned hot in a heartbeat.

For one magical second, she forgot to be afraid and simply surrendered to the longings that drew her to him.

Sensing it, he parted her lips roughly and deepened the kiss, ravaging her mouth, claiming it until the heat took them both to that precarious edge.

His chest heaving, he groaned, then released her.

"You didn't like it?" she asked, surprised that he'd let go of her.

"Like it?" He swore softly. "Woman, I want to seduce you right here, right now. The ground beneath us is hard, but I promise that, after a moment, all you'd feel is me giving you pleasure."

His words left her weak at the knees and aware of everything about him. His face was tense, his body hard. He was ready, and holding back was nearly killing him.

Temptation shimmered in the air, whispering of needs as old as time. Desire tightened its hold on her.

He ran his index finger down the side of her face, then traced her parted lips. "Just one yes and I'll make the desert sunrise brighter than the noonday sun. I'll show you the power of a touch and make you melt against me."

His voice caressed her, sparking her senses. She licked her lips, her mouth dry, her body thrumming with needs too powerful to ignore. "I…"

Hearing the hesitation in her voice, he took another step back. "You're not ready." He took a deep breath. "Have you ever…"

"I'm not a virgin, if that's what you mean—not that there have been many men," she added. "When I was younger, I experimented, thinking casual sex would be enough. It never was, not for me. After the glow faded, it left me feeling cold and more alone than ever." She paused, struggling to find the right words. "It was like being given a glimpse into paradise, only to be told I didn't meet the requirements and couldn't stay."

He nodded slowly. "Go get your things. I'll wait for you here, then I'll lock up the house."

She started to say something else, but words failed her. There wasn't anything more to say. She wasn't ready to take their relationship to the next step and maybe never would be. Fear and love couldn't coexist, and, for now, fear had the upper hand.

Chapter Ten

Lori sat behind the counter at the DMV, trying to stop thinking about Gene so she could concentrate on her work. When he'd dropped her off at work at nine, she'd thought that putting some distance between them would help her think clearly again. So far, that hadn't worked.

After the early rush settled, she was ready for some coffee and, having arrived on time, still had a break coming. As she went inside the break room she saw that Miranda was already there.

"Hey, pregnant lady," Lori said and smiled.

"Hey, yourself. I've been dying to talk to you! So tell me all about what's going on with you and the hunk. I saw him drop you off. Did you spend a wild Friday night with him?" Before Lori could answer, Miranda's eyes lit up and she smiled. "Aha! Of course you did! That's why you've got that look on your face. You're almost sparkling! Did you have wild sex with him? Fess up and tell me *everything!*"

Lori nearly choked, then glanced around, making

sure no one else could hear them. "I haven't gone to bed with him. He's helping me, that's all."

Miranda looked crestfallen. "You really should hook up. He's hot and he's really into you. I saw him watching you after he dropped you off this morning and—" Miranda suddenly stopped speaking, her eyes narrowing. "Wait one second. Are you telling me that you spent the night with him and *nothing* happened? Either you're holding out on me or something's seriously wrong."

Lori burst out laughing. "Nothing's wrong with him or me. We spent the night together, but in separate rooms."

"But that's not the way you really wanted it to be, is it?" She studied her friend's expression closely, then smiled. "You're crazy about him, so why fight it? You need more from life than weekends fixing up your house, girlfriend. Grab that cowboy by his silver belt buckle and seduce the heck out of him. I bet he'll give you the ride of your life."

Lori burst out laughing. It was too outrageous to react any other way. "I'll keep that in mind."

"Good. Here's what you do. Fantasize about what you want him to do to you, then what you'll do to him. Let that simmer until you can't think of anything else, then jump him."

"That's your hormones talking, girl," Lori said, chuckling. "They're making you crazy."

"Even if that's true, I'm still right."

Once her break ended, Lori walked back across

the long section of desks and office space that was located behind the counter. As she passed one of the workstations, Lori saw Steve staring at his monitor, cursing just loud enough for her to hear.

He looked up, a scowl on his face, and she gave him a sympathetic smile. Poor Steve. He'd always been the slowest among them when it came to processing customers. She was almost sure that it wasn't deliberate. He was just inept when it came to the software they used at the DMV. She saw him stand up, still scowling at the computer.

"Can I help with something, Steve?" she asked.

"Nah, thanks. I just needed to look something up." He walked over to the bookcase behind Jerry's unoccupied desk and pulled out a computer manual.

Lori hurried to her own workstation, and as she settled in she heard a faint metallic scrape on the window glass to the right of the foyer entrance. She turned her head to look, and what she saw took her by complete surprise.

For a second, all she could do was stare. Gene was outside in a gray uniform shirt, tan cap and matching slacks, cleaning the glass with a squeegee.

He smiled at her, then shook his head slightly and returned to his work.

Lori took the hint and turned away. As she called the next waiting customer, she smiled. Gene had undoubtedly pulled strings so he could substitute for the minimall's regular window washer. From his position above the DMV floor, he'd be able to spot anyone fitting Bud Harrington's description and alert Harvey immediately.

Just then Steve came up from behind and tapped her on the shoulder. The first thing she noted was that he looked furious.

"Lori, I need your help. I've been trying to access the DMV state database, but when I enter my password, I keep getting an invalid password flag." He ran an exasperated hand over his face. "I even tried it from the boss's workstation. It's nuts. I *know* my own password."

"You're trying to access a restricted database. That's why it's happening. The system's set up that way to prevent anyone without clearance from downloading the entire state file, which includes every registered owner's personal information. We only have access on a per individual basis—if you already have their social, tag number, registration number, address or telephone number. Your password won't let you conduct any kind of data search without one of those parameters. We'd catch hell if we started data mining or downloading, and there's a keystroke recording program that picks up on activity like that. What was it you were looking for? Maybe there's another way to get it."

"It's a little tricky. A client came in, said he wanted to renew his license, then wanted to know if I'd look up his ex-wife's social security number for some legal papers he had with him and needed to file today. All he wanted was verification, so I told him I'd see what I could do. Unfortunately, he didn't know her new last name—she'd remarried."

"It's a good thing you didn't get into the system, or you would have been in a world of hurt. Jerry would have caught hell, too, if that had been tracked back to his computer. With the recent outbreak of identity thefts in this area, anything that could compromise the personal information of our customers has to be carefully monitored. We just can't afford to bend the rules for anyone these days."

Steve shook his head and shrugged. "The guy's harmless. Take a look for yourself," he said, then turned and pointed to his station. "Crap. He split."

"He must have been up to something and you got off lucky," she said. "Can you describe him?" She wasn't sure if she was acting paranoid or not, but she wanted to make sure the incident hadn't somehow been connected to Bud Harrington.

"There was nothing particularly noteworthy about him. He was Hispanic, average height, muscular build, dark hair, dark eyes. He was dressed in jeans and some kind of work jacket, blue, no company logo."

"Do you remember his name?"

"Yeah, Mark Jaramillo, and his supposed ex-wife's name was Juanita. Do you think he was an illegal trolling for social security numbers, or something like that?"

"It's possible," she said. "You might want to enter it in your logbook, or make a note of it for Jerry."

"Good idea, thanks."

As Steve returned to his station, she used her cell phone to call Gene.

"Your local window washer here," he answered.

She laughed. "How on earth did you get that job? Did you bribe one of your brothers?"

"Something like that. Sparkly Windows, which services this mall, also cleans Dan's office. He got them to let me take the regular guy's place this morning. Just don't give me away."

"That's why I'm calling instead of talking to you directly," she said, and told him what had just happened.

"Several guys fitting that general description have walked in and out the last fifteen minutes or so, but no one was acting suspicious or I would have noticed," he said. "I also haven't seen Harrington, or any light-haired, slender, tall Anglo male."

"Okay, thanks. I better get back to work."

She'd never had anyone care enough to want to protect her as Gene did. The thought filled her with a special warmth. She could definitely get used to having him around.

THE REST OF THE MORNING WENT by quickly. Even with clients rushing in to beat the half-day schedule, her thoughts always drifted back to Gene—where he was, whether he was thinking of her and, inevitably, how long he'd stick around Hartley. As far back as she could remember, no one she'd ever cared about had stayed around for long.

It was twelve-fifteen when she left the building. Steve had remained behind to lock up, Harvey with him. At least Steve had one friend at work. He seemed like such a loner at times.

As she walked to the parking area, Gene pulled up immediately, reaching across the pickup to open the passenger door for her.

She smiled and climbed into his truck. "I see you've given up the Jeep and your fabulous weekend job as window washer," she teased, noting his change of clothes and cowboy hat.

He laughed.

"Will you take a quick drive past my house? I want to make sure everything's okay there," she said, fastening her seat belt.

"Sure." They were stopped at a light when he spoke again. "I've been giving a lot of thought to what's been happening to you, and I have an idea, something we haven't considered before. The break-in at Preston's happened when you weren't even there. If all the incidents are related, then that means this guy may not necessarily be after you personally, but rather after something you have."

"That doesn't make any sense to me. The most valuable thing I've purchased recently is my paint sprayer," she said and saw him smile.

"Think harder," he said. "Let's say we're on the right track. What could you possibly have that someone else is willing to risk everything to get? Do you go to garage sales, estate sales or any other place where you might have bought something that someone else just had to have? I'm thinking of a family heirloom, a vase worth thousands of dollars, a small wooden box with money hidden inside— anything along those lines?"

She shook her head. "Sorry. None of the above. The only things I've bought recently are a used re- frigerator and some small tools I needed to fix up my house. I'm not big on nostalgia, which describes a lot of collectors. Generally, they're searching for things that evoke memories, but that's not me. I'm more focused on the future, and my present is a work in progress. My past…is over."

"All right, then. For now, we'll rule out anything you may have brought home recently." He grew silent, then after several seconds spoke again. "The subject of collectors seems to have struck a nerve with you."

She nodded slowly. "It brought back an old memory. My mom had a huge collection of family photos and a gazillion souvenirs from our family vacations. We had shelves and shelves of those at home. Then one morning I found her tossing every- thing on those shelves into the trash. Everything that had something to do with the past went out with the garbage."

"Did you ever figure out what happened between them?"

"To this day I'm still not sure, but I think Mom may have fallen in love with someone else. She got married a few months afterward and, before long, started traveling all over the world with her husband, an army colonel. He had no interest in children, and considering they were always on the go, Mom said I'd be better off staying stateside with Dad, who was a salesman for a local tool company. It made sense, but I couldn't help but feel that she chose her new life with him over me," Lori said. "To Dad, I was a reminder of Mom, so he didn't want to be around me, particularly after he remarried."

"They went on with their lives, but you couldn't fit in anywhere." Seeing her nod, he added, "So you pulled away from everyone?"

"Pretty much," she said.

She took a shaky breath and then smiled as Gene squeezed her hand gently. "The day I turned eighteen, I packed up, left and never looked back." She gave him a thin smile. "So you see, having a family isn't necessarily what it's made out to be."

"In some ways, we're two of a kind. The circumstances were different, but we both took it on the chin before we knew how to block a punch," he said. "You've been on your own since?"

"Yeah, and I've been able to handle every crisis and turning point in my life—till now. If you hadn't come along, I would have been looking for a place to hide, or maybe I would have just cut and run."

"No, you wouldn't have done either. You're too much of a fighter."

She smiled. "Yeah, you're right, but it's still nice to have a friend you can count on."

THEY WERE SOON AT HER HOUSE. Lori stopped by the mailbox long enough to pick up its contents, then insisted on checking the interior of the house. Everything seemed all right to him, but he could tell something was bothering her.

Once they were back in his truck, he glanced over at her. "What's wrong?"

She smiled. "So you're into mind reading, too?"

"Nah. You're just not much of a poker player. When you're worried it's always right there on your face," he said as they got under way.

"I've been thinking about your idea that my stalker's not so much interested in me as in something he thinks I have," she said. "If you're right, then he's bound to come back here. Will you help me stake out my house, at least for a while?"

"Sure, but that'll mean long hours sitting in this truck."

"I know. So let me buy us some good fast food. Cheap Eats is nearby and their megaburgers are out of this world."

"You like that place?" he asked, surprised. "That sign of theirs is something else."

She laughed. "You mean the roadrunner chasing

the running hamburger? I think that's why it attracts a young crowd. They see the humor."

"Madam, are you intimating that I'm old?" he said, feigning outrage.

She laughed even harder. "No," she said, then, growing serious, added, "but you have old-fashioned, traditional male values."

"Is that a bad thing?"

"Not at all. In fact, if you feel I'm infringing on traditional male territory, I'd be happy to let you buy dinner for us."

He laughed. "I walked into that."

"Yep, you did."

THEY SAT IN THE CAB OF GENE'S pickup, across the street and one house down from her home, just out of sight of her neighbor's window. After taking a quick look through Lori's backyard, Gene insisted she call Mrs. Hopgood and let her know they were there. That way her elderly neighbor wouldn't call the police, and they'd avoid a face-off with a tired cop responding to a suspicious-vehicle call.

Lori held out her French fries. "Take some. These are the best fries in the county."

He shook his head. "Thanks, but no."

"Who doesn't like French fries?"

"I like them a lot better when they're not dripping in oil."

"It's peanut oil, and that's what makes them so good," she said, finishing the last of them in one large bite. "Of course, this will cost me big-time. Tomorrow's lunch will probably be a granola bar."

"Then you'll be starving by dinner."

"Yes, but with luck, you'll buy again."

"Nah. Next time you're getting the bill. I'm just a working man," he said, chuckling, then reached for his cell phone. "I'm thinking I should take another walk through your backyard, but first I'll call Dan and let him know what we're doing."

"Just in case?"

"Yeah. Dan doesn't live far from here and I know he'll back me up if necessary. I haven't called him in before now because he's got a new wife and he's also been working some long hours on a job for the tribe. He's had his hands full, but he'll come through for me."

When Daniel answered the telephone call, Gene brought him up to speed.

"I heard from Paul before he left town. He told me you might call and put me on standby after telling me he wouldn't be back till this evening," Dan said. "He warned me that the lady's *hot* and that's scrambling your thinking."

"Then what's your excuse?"

Daniel laughed loudly.

"Just stand by, bro. I don't expect trouble, but—"

"Gotcha. If you find it, the cavalry is minutes away."

Gene hung up, then noted the way Lori was looking at him. From her expression it looked to him as if she was trying to make up her mind about something. If she'd heard Dan's comment... "Did you catch any of that?"

"No, was I supposed to?"

"Nah, it was just some teasing. My brothers and I always give each other a hard time."

"When you all get together, what do you like to do? Watch sports, talk cars and trucks, drink beer or all of the above?"

He had started to answer when he spotted movement. Someone was coming out of the backyard via a side gate. "Over there by the juniper bush, left side."

She followed his line of sight and saw a shadowy figure standing next to the wall.

"He must have come in through the alley. We've got him!" Lori dove for the door handle.

"No, wait!" His warning came too late. The instant the intruder heard the truck door open, he fled back through the gate into the backyard.

Gene shot past Lori, raced across the front lawn and spotted the person near the back fence.

The intruder cleared the three-foot-high fence with a scissors jump, then raced down the alley, which was lined with backyard fences and a cinder-block wall on the opposite side.

Gene cleared the fence a heartbeat later, then chased the running man to the end of the block. The guy sprinted across the street, then ran up the outside steps of a three-story office building. The place was constructed to look like an old mountain resort, with planters dangling from the roofs of the covered walkways.

Gene reached the steps seconds later, then ran up, taking two at a time. Although he lost visual contact with the man for a moment, once on the first landing he heard the guy's footsteps ahead on the wooden walkway.

At the top of the flight of stairs, Gene caught a fresh glimpse of the man now sprinting past the office doors. The guy took the corner of the L-shaped building on the fly, grabbing a corner post to keep his balance as he whipped around the turn.

Though fifty feet away, Gene heard the man's labored breathing. Gene slowly closed the gap, knowing that he had the stamina to stay in the chase for as long as it took.

The walkway ended at another stairway. This time the running man headed down, descending with a rumble of quick steps.

When Gene suddenly heard the shift of heavy steps on the sidewalk below, he realized that the man had reversed directions. Worried that the guy would meet up with Lori, Gene made it down the stairs in three quick leaps.

Looking ahead, Gene could see the man, wearing a Scorpions jacket, suddenly turn right and run between the buildings.

Gene breathed with relief. Good, he'd never run into Lori going that way.

At the corner, Gene saw the minimall directly ahead. It had two levels of enclosed shops forming a big U, with the parking lot in the middle. Gene slowed and glanced around. He'd lost sight of the man again, but the closest entrance door was just closing.

Gene had stepped off the curb when he heard the blast of a horn and saw the headlights of an approaching car.

"Use the crosswalk, moron!" a man yelled from inside the passing car as it raced past him.

"Wait for me!" a gasping voice called to Gene from behind. He turned his head and saw Lori running toward him. In half a beat, she caught up to him and they crossed the street together.

"He's in the mall somewhere," Gene said. "Stick with me."

Once inside, they saw at least fifty shoppers up and down the main walkway, but most of the people were looking in the opposite direction. One woman bent down to retrieve a dropped package.

"Where did the guy in the Scorpions jacket go? He picked my pocket," Gene yelled out.

"That way, dude," a heavyweight teenage boy answered almost immediately, pointing.

Gene and Lori hurried to the end of the wide hall, bypassing the shoppers, who gave them room and shouted encouragement. When they turned the corner, they saw someone with the right color jacket getting into the elevator at the end of the passage.

Gene let go of her hand and raced to the door, hitting the button just as the door slid shut. Frustrated, he banged his fist on the metal, then turned and headed for the stairs.

Out of nowhere, the high-pitched wail of an alarm sounded, and strobe lights on the wall above the red fire alarm began to flash.

Within seconds people were rushing out of the shops and hurrying toward the exits.

"Everyone outside!" a shout came from somewhere behind them. "Take the stairs, not the elevator."

Gene turned and saw a uniformed security guard motioning to shoppers.

"We're screwed. Let's go," Gene said, taking Lori's hand and heading toward the nearest exit.

"You think the fire alarm was his doing?" Lori asked, still trying to catch her breath.

"Count on it."

Chapter Eleven

On the way back to his car Gene called Daniel and gave him Lori's address. "Can you make sure he doesn't head back to her house and try to surprise us there? We'll be going back to take a look around and figure out what he was up to, but there's a lot of confusion and traffic here now and we might be a while."

"You've got it. I'll be there in less than a minute. I started heading your way right after you called," Dan said.

As they got under way, Lori gave Gene a worried look. "What if your brother gets there well ahead of us and runs into a problem?"

"Daniel can handle it."

"Alone?" she said, her voice rising.

"The guy will be in a world of trouble if he decides to square off with Dan. My brother's trained to fight. Daniel was in the army and he loves a challenge."

"What are you saying, that he likes to fight?"

"No, not exactly. Dan, like the rest of us, has to

test himself from time to time. We all came from hard backgrounds and know only the tough survive. That's why we like making sure we haven't gotten too soft and lost our edge." He shrugged. "It's a guy thing."

"But you're not a fighter. You're a gentle man. You weigh your actions and don't get hostile unless you're provoked."

"Not always. I have another side, one you haven't seen. You know that Bear is my spiritual brother. Bear can be good, but it can also be evil when it's not under control. *Hosteen* Silver understood this— that's why he gave me the bear fetish to carry with me in my medicine pouch. He knew Bear and I are linked."

She looked at him thoughtfully. She couldn't imagine Gene having a dark side. He took life in measured strides, was slow to anger and wasn't afraid to stand up for what he thought was right, even when it came at a cost. She knew all that from personal experience.

These days when everyone's lives were so rushed, when people went from one thing to another with scarcely a breath in between, it was remarkable to find a man like Gene.

When his phone rang, Gene placed it on speaker. Dan's familiar voice came through. "We're too late. The back door was forced by twisting off the knob with some kind of wrench. I didn't go inside, but from what I can see, the place has been ransacked.

I don't think the guy's still inside, but if he is, he's not going anywhere. I'll make sure of it. I've also called the police, and they'll be sending a man out."

"Yeah, when, next year?" she muttered, but both men heard her.

"Don't give up," Dan said.

"I'm not. I'm just angry. I want this guy caught and locked up."

After ending the call, Gene glanced over at her. "He couldn't have done this since leaving the mall. He must have gotten inside while we were watching from the front. I should have parked where we had a better angle and increased the number of times I went around the house on foot."

"We couldn't be everywhere at once and there was no sign of an intruder from where we were. But why did he break in at all?"

"Have you thought some more about what you might have in your possession that could be so important to this guy?" Gene asked. "It wouldn't necessarily have to be something of economic value. Has anyone sent you anything they might want back, like love letters, incriminating emails or anything of that nature?"

"No, I've got nothing along those lines." She thought about it for several long moments. "Last week I borrowed a book that belongs to my friend Miranda. All of us at the office wanted to read it, so Miranda passed it around. I was the fourth woman in line for it. Right now it's at the house."

"Is it possible that something's hidden inside it?"

"I doubt it, or one of the three ladies who read it before me would have found it."

"Unless one of them, or a member of their families, placed it in there," he said. "Is it a hardcover with a thick spine that could contain something?"

She shook her head. "It's a sexy paperback romance novel."

He gave her a thoroughly masculine grin. "I would have never guessed you like to read those. You seem pretty down-to-earth."

"What's one got to do with the other? I love romance novels with happy endings. They're fun to read and they make you feel good." She smiled slowly. "Did I mention that the hero's a Navajo?"

He burst out laughing. "I'm no hero, so if you expect me to be like him you're bound to be disappointed."

"Not so far," she said, smiling.

As they drove up her street, her playful mood vanished. "How bad do you think it'll be inside my place?"

"We'll find out soon enough." Gene pulled up behind Daniel's pickup, which was parked at the curb in front of her driveway.

Lori pointed to the empty police car across the street. "That was fast. Either Dan's got some serious clout, or the slowdown's finally over."

"It's probably Dan. He's made some good friends

in the department, and they're there for him when he calls."

"I'm impressed."

"Should I be jealous?" Gene asked.

"Nah, I prefer the company I keep," she said as she climbed out of the truck.

Gene soon introduced Lori to his brother.

Dan shook her hand. As Lori turned away to glance at her home, Dan gave his brother a quick thumbs-up.

"Have you been inside?" Lori asked Dan, turning back.

"No, Officer Green is in there now taking a look around. From what I saw through the rear window, some of the rooms are in shambles, so be prepared."

She stepped up to the front window and, seeing the officer walking around, called out to him. "Can I come in? I've got my keys."

"Yeah," Green said, motioning with his hand.

Anxious to put an end to her speculation, Lori unlocked the front door and stepped inside.

As SHE DISAPPEARED FROM VIEW, Dan blocked Gene's way, forcing him to hang back for a minute longer. "I see what got you into this mess."

"No, you don't," Gene snapped.

"Sure I do. A beautiful woman like that smiles and soon all you can think about is how good that sexy little body would feel beneath yours."

"Wash your mouth and brain out with soap. Better yet, maybe I'll do it for you."

Dan laughed. "Oh, yeah. It's serious."

Gene glared at him. "I'm trying to help her out. This woman's got a big problem on her hands."

"Yeah—you," Dan said, grinning. "You'd take on a bar full of bikers just to see her smile. Tell me I'm wrong," he said. Gene glowered at him and Dan added, "She's got you, bro."

"This coming from someone who already crashed and burned," Gene snarled, then went inside.

Lori was in the living room. "Officer, this guy is a total nut job. I have absolutely no idea why he's doing this to me!" Lori looked around in shock. "How long was he in here?"

"This wouldn't take long—maybe five minutes tops. To me, it looks like he was searching for something specific," the officer said. "Take a close look around. His search pattern might give you an indication of what he's after."

With Gene right behind her, Lori slowly walked through the house. All the drawers, everything from the ones in the kitchen to the ones in the other rooms, had been taken out and upended. The bookcases had also been emptied and her books were scattered all around the carpet. Her couch cushions had been removed and now rested atop the mess. Even her trash had been dumped into the bathtub and sorted through.

"He really is convinced that I'm hiding something," she said.

"Are you?" the young officer pressed.

"No, and after this he's got to see that, too," she said.

Gene shook his head. "He might have found whatever it was. It's also possible that he didn't and is now convinced that you've got whatever it is on you."

As Lori glanced at the three men, she saw curiosity in their eyes. "Guys, all I've got that he hasn't seen or searched thoroughly are my clothes and this handbag. He tried to grab my purse before—if Gene and I are right and it was the same man—but he lost it during the chase." Seeing the uncertainty on their faces, she knew they weren't convinced. They still thought she knew something. "Let's clear this up right now."

Lori slipped the purse off her shoulder and dumped the contents on the floor. "Lipstick, compact, keys, penlight, breath mints, ID badge, pad and pencil, my wallet." She unsnapped that and opened it for them. "Fifteen dollars in cash—no hidden sections. My credit card, driver's license and a medical insurance card." She stepped back. "Normally I also carry my laptop, but it's in my overnight case right now inside Gene's truck. This guy obviously has me mixed up with someone else. There's no other answer."

To her surprise, the police officer came to take a

closer look at the contents of her handbag. "Nothing," he said at last.

She placed everything back into her purse. "I'll keep looking through the house and see if I can come up with any answers."

Bracing herself, Lori entered the bedroom and froze just inside the doorway. Her throat felt so tight she could barely breathe, and even though she was trying hard to be brave, she could feel tears stinging her eyes. Refusing to blink, she stared at the mess before her. Even her underwear drawer had been upended and searched through.

Lori picked up all her panties and bras, then dumped them into the trash.

"Just wash them," Gene said, loud enough for only her to hear.

"No, there's not enough disinfectant in this world to make me wear what he touched," she said. "*Why* won't he leave me alone?" she added, her voice wavering.

"The answers are inside you," Gene said, "but you're too close to this to see them."

"I agree with Gene," Daniel said, coming up to join them. "The officer tried lifting prints off a few surfaces the intruder clearly touched but, so far, he's gotten nowhere. It looks like the guy was wearing gloves. On some level, I'm betting that you know what's going on."

"I've done nothing but think about this. I have no answers. The only thing I know for sure right now is that I need to clean up this mess," she said, looking around her home and trying to hold herself together. If she started crying now, she'd never be able to stop. "Maybe something will come to me as I do that."

"We'll help," Gene said, then pointed to her old desktop computer. "It doesn't look like he touched that. It's still off."

"It's practically a relic, and not even hooked up anymore. I use my laptop when I blog and surf the internet. I've got to say I wish that it had been here for him to take." She held up a CD software jacket. "I've got a tracking program installed. If he'd powered it up, we could have hunted him down."

Daniel nodded. "Smart move. That's a good security measure."

She stepped over closer to her desk. "He didn't touch my desktop computer, but my software storage has been ransacked," she said, pointing to the cubbyhole on the left-hand side of the desk. "My backup flash drives are all over the floor, too. He also rummaged through the top desk drawer and the shelves beneath the desk."

"Odd, considering his lack of interest in your computer. It's an unusual home intrusion," the officer said, walking into the room. "This wasn't the work of an ordinary thief. Whoever did this was either looking for something specific, out to intimidate you or both."

"Only one person fits the bill, Officer Green,"

she said. "Bud Harrington. He wants me to live in fear, not knowing what might happen next. To him, it's payback for the complaint I filed against him. I probably stirred him up, too, when I spoke to him the other day and told him to back off. He insisted on acting like the injured party, so it got me no-where."

"But Harrington hasn't been at his house in days," Gene said, reminding her.

"He still answers his business phone, so I'm guessing he's staying with a friend in town or maybe has a second home somewhere nearby." She paused and looked at each of the men. "The answer I'm giving you may not be what you want, but it's the only one I have."

"We'll do our best to follow it up," the officer said.

Dan motioned to Officer Green. "Come on, I'll walk you to the door."

As they left, Lori continued picking up. "Very few things have actually been damaged," she said.

Gene retrieved a paperback from the floor next to the bed. "*Spirit Warrior*. Is this the book you men-tioned?" Gene studied the cover that showcased a shirtless Native American man riding a horse, with a buxom, long-haired blonde hottie clinging to him.

"Yeah." She looked down at the cover, then back up at him. "Come to think of it, he does look a bit like you."

Dan came back into the room, glanced at the

cover, then at his brother, and laughed. "You took the words right out of my mouth, Lori, but Gene's got more muscles. You noticed that, right?"

"Will you excuse us?" Gene said, then hauled his brother by the back of his shirt into the next room.

She couldn't hear what the guys were saying, just muffled voices. Chuckling, she looked down at the cover again. Daniel was right. Gene was definitely broader in the chest and better looking all around, though she hadn't seen him shirtless yet.

Even as the thought formed, she pushed it back. *Yet?* Was she losing her mind? It had to be the result of overexposure to testosterone. She shoved the book into her purse.

Gene came back into the room minutes later and started helping her put the software CDs back in their place.

"The back door was kicked in and badly splintered, basically ruined," Dan said, joining them. "It can be screwed shut and secured for tonight, but it can't be used. You shouldn't stay here until you can update and change all the locks, and also replace the back door."

"We've been using the house in Copper Canyon," she said.

Dan looked at his brother in surprise, then shook his head. "That may not be such a good idea. Cell phones are iffy up there, and the landline goes out every time there's a storm. Your ranch, on the other hand..." he said, letting the thought hang.

"You're right," Gene said. "I've been wanting to get back to Two Springs Ranch to check on my animals, too. Devon, my neighbor's son, does a good job, but there's still a lot going on during spring, so I'd like to keep a closer eye on things." Gene looked at Lori. "What do you say?"

"Where, exactly, is your ranch?" Lori asked.

"Southern Colorado, about a ninety-minute drive from here. Since the DMV won't be open again till Monday, there won't be any problem getting back in time."

"But my house—that back door," she reminded him.

"Security is what I do," Dan said. "If you leave me a key, I'll seal the place up tight tonight, then make sure people I trust come by tomorrow and get it all fixed up for you. I'll pay them, and you can settle up with me later."

"How expensive will it be?"

"As long as you choose the same grade and style door that's on there now, probably not so much, though the labor will be extra, it being Sunday," Daniel said. "I may be able to get you an upgrade, too, because most companies deal wholesale with me."

"Then do it, but if they don't take credit cards, I may have to make payments. Will that be a problem?"

"Nah. Gene trusts you, which means so do I."

"Thanks," she said and smiled. "I really appreciate what you're doing for me," Lori said, then glanced at Gene. "I'd love to get out of town for the weekend, and staying at your ranch sounds just about perfect."

"Then it's a go," Gene said.

Lori gathered up a few more essentials in a large tote bag and was ready.

"I gather from what you said before that you like horses?" Gene said, walking back outside with her. Dan was nearby, getting tools from his truck.

"Yeah, I love them. I used to work at a stable when I was in high school just so I could ride free of charge."

He smiled. "I have a gelding you might like."

"Don't let him rope you into mucking out the stalls. Remind him you're a guest," Dan teased as he came over to say goodbye.

Gene gave Daniel a not-too-gentle slap on the head, then glanced back at Lori. "If there's anything else from the house you'd like to take with you, now's your chance."

She glanced back at the house. It would take time—and plenty of locks and alarms—before she'd feel completely safe there again. Holding up her tote, she said, "I'm good to go when you are."

She climbed into the truck, eager to leave. Visiting Gene's home would give her a chance to see his world close-up. If she found that she couldn't share his love for Two Springs Ranch, then she'd know for sure that their closeness was temporary and eventually would come to an end.

Chapter Twelve

The familiar drive took them to Shiprock, then north past tall, slender rock formations reminiscent of Monument Valley. After that, they passed the Colorado state line and were off the Navajo Nation. Twice, Gene saw a pickup following them, but both times, the vehicle eventually turned away.

Moving into higher terrain dotted with junipers and piñon trees, they soon entered the city of Cortez, then continued northeast out of the city. There were low rolling hills dotted with more junipers and pines among fields of dryland grasses and future alfalfa crops.

Here, moisture was much more abundant, but only by comparison. The true forests remained north and east where the Colorado Plateau was crowned by the San Juan Mountains.

Taking a narrow, paved state road, they drove across open country punctuated by stretches of wire fence and an occasional ranch or farm. Cattle and horses grazed peacefully over the open range. Soon they went down a dusty dirt road and after an eternity reached a big metal gate.

About a half mile beyond that, Lori caught glimpses of three or four buildings and a large red barn. There were several fruit groves and, higher up the hill, outlying pines of the encroaching forest.

"I'll get the gate," Gene said. "Will you drive the truck through so I can lock up behind us?"

"Lock? I don't see one. Where is it?"

"See that square metal box? The lock's inside. That way no one can get at it with bolt cutters. Only the right code on the keypad will work. Daniel came up with the design. He has a similar system on the gate outside his business."

Gene opened the gate, then, after locking back up, joined her. "It'll be hard for anyone to sneak up on us here. It's mostly open ground and there's crunchy gravel farther up, closer to the house."

"I can't wait to see everything!"

GENE PARKED NEAR THE MAIN house, then glanced at Lori, studying her expression. "What I see when I look at this ranch and what others see can be vastly different," he said slowly. "My cattle and horses are my pride and future. To my brothers, Paul and Dan in particular, Two Springs Ranch is about animals that need to be fed and cared for and lots of backbreaking work."

"What *you* think is all that matters," she said. "This place fills you with a sense of purpose. More importantly, it's what you love. As they say, never mess with a winning game."

"Truer words were never spoken. Two Springs Ranch is everything I ever wanted and more," he said, standing by the truck and looking out at the pasture. "I make a good living when things are going well, but money isn't at the heart of why I stay. No one in ranching ever gets paid enough to make up for the long hours and the uncertainty that's built into it. When times are tough, just getting through the day can be hard, but the land and the cattle will always put food on the table. I've never once doubted that this is where I belong, and that this is a life worth living. It all comes down to what matters most and pushing the rest aside."

"I understand exactly how you feel."

"Do you?" he pressed.

She nodded. "It's all about passion, really. This ranch and the life you lead here is the food your soul needs."

"Yes, that's it exactly. I couldn't have said it better myself." As he looked at her, he realized just how much her opinion of the ranch mattered to him. For a man who'd never given a damn how others saw him, that was a first. "Let me show you around."

He led her to the main house. "All the buildings except the barn are structured log-cabin style because they're cool in summer and warm in winter. I've added modern touches, too, such as floor insulation, to save energy. I've got high-efficiency wood-burning stoves inside and maintain my own sustainable woodlot. That saves on propane."

As he opened the front door and showed her inside, she smiled, her eyes huge and bright. She looked at the shelves that held his sports trophies and rodeo awards. She then walked to the west wall and admired his Southwestern landscapes featuring wild animals and horses.

"I love your place. It's strong, masculine, yet friendly and peaceful all at the same time."

As she walked around the main room, she stopped by the two couches with stained log frames. She gave a cursory glance to the wall-mounted flat-screen TV, but lingered by the wood coffee table with its inlaid Mexican tile top.

"I built the shelves and carved most of the furniture myself. Those were things I learned from *Hosteen* Silver. The cushions on the couch and the Navajo rug are the work of a Navajo woman who lives about thirty miles south of here."

"The place looks rugged...like you," she said.

He smiled. He could live with that. "Let me show you the rest of the house."

He led her down the hall. "My office," he said, showing her a room with a simple oak desk in the center, a pine swivel chair behind it and two tall bookcases against the side walls. Each was filled with books on ranching, agriculture and accounting. There were a handful of thrillers there, too, and dozens of paperback Westerns.

"What, no romance novels?"

"Haven't tried any of those, but maybe I will. You never know. I might get a few pointers."

"I suspect you don't need any," she said, hiding a smile.

Lori went to the window and looked at the huge, open field dotted with pines that lay just beyond. "When you're taking care of the business side of ranching, this view must help you keep things in perspective."

"That's why I chose this room as my office. Ranching is a tough business, not just a fantasy of the Old West," he said. "They say that if you love what you do, you'll never work a day in your life, but I guess that doesn't apply to ranching."

Next, he showed her a guest bedroom. There was a plain white bedspread on the full-size bed, and blinds on the windows. A large chest of drawers stood against one wall, and a pine wardrobe against the other.

"My brothers use this room when they come," he said. "Of course, if more than one of them shows up, I provide sleeping bags. I've also got a bunk-house—a throwback to another era—that'll eventually house all of them, but for the time being it's a work in progress."

He walked to the doorway and waved toward the last room down the hall. "That's my bedroom."

Peering inside, Lori's attention was immediately

captured by the full-size four-poster bed. Then, just as he'd suspected, the quilted bedspread caught her eye.

As he followed her gaze, he saw her take in each of the squares. They were defined by an array of blues, some floral designs, others solids. Each was embroidered with tiny stitches that made up intricate patterns.

"That's the most gorgeous quilt I've ever seen," she said.

"My mother made it for me when I was a kid. It's the only thing I've kept of the old days before *Hosteen* Silver stepped into my life. It's to remind me that there's beauty in everyone's life, though sometimes we don't see it until it's too late."

"What happened to your parents?" she asked softly.

"Alcoholism ruined our family. It cost us everything, including my parents' lives. They got behind the wheel one afternoon and never made it home."

"I'm so sorry," she said, reaching for his hand.

"Don't be. There's good even in bad times. I grew stronger because of the way I was raised, and I learned to stand on my own. The situation at home eventually led me to *Hosteen* Silver, too, and a new family."

Lori went up and put her arms around him, giving him a hug. "I wish I had your strength," she said.

"You have it, Lori—along with me," he said, then lowered his mouth to hers.

She sighed softly and pressed herself against him. Feeling her softness melting into him, he sucked in a breath. "You're too tempting," he said, then, with a low groan, eased his hold and stepped away.

"*I'm* tempting?" she said. "That's exactly the way I'd describe *you*."

He held her gaze, searching her eyes. "Some people spend their whole lives searching for what we've found."

"I need to be sure it's something I really want," she said in a whisper-thin voice.

He touched her cheek with his palm, his thumb caressing her tenderly.

"Mr. Redhouse?" a booming voice suddenly called out from the front room.

Startled, Lori jumped back.

Gene took a breath and cursed. "My neighbor's son. He's staying in the bunkhouse. I fixed up one of the rooms in there for him."

"Hey, Devon," Gene called out, walking down the hall. "How have things been going here?"

"Great—if you don't count Grit," he said with a grin, shaking Gene's hand enthusiastically.

As Lori came up Gene introduced her. "Lori, this is Devon Portman. He'll be going off to college next year and leaving me without the best ranch hand I've ever had."

Devon, a blond kid about seventeen in worn jeans and a battered straw hat, smiled at her and offered his hand.

She shook it. "Pleasure."

"It's like I keep telling my dad," he said, glancing back at Gene. "I'm not meant for college."

"What is it that you want to do?" Lori asked him.

"I'm a rancher, ma'am, like my dad and his dad before him. Dad says that he doesn't want his son to have to work with his back all day, but that's the life I want."

"Then go to Colorado State and major in something like agriculture, veterinary medicine or even accounting. You'll need more than sweat to make things work in a ranch," Gene said. "Education never hurts, son."

"That's what I keep hearing."

"So what's been happening around here?" Gene asked.

"Two calves were born, and Ace showed signs of colic day before yesterday. The vet came out and Ace is doing fine now and back on his feed." He stared at his boots for a few moments.

"What's on your mind?" Gene pressed.

"Someone's hanging around the property, sir. I noticed him on the way up here. I was working the fence line along the west pasture when I saw an old green pickup parked down the road. He was checking out the front gate, like he was searching for the lock. When I started walking over, he saw me and drove off."

"Maybe he was just checking out my brother's

handiwork. Did you recognize the truck?" Gene asked him.

"No, but the old Johnson place has new owners, and it could have been one of them, I guess. I spoke to Dad about it, and he said I should pass it along to you. There haven't been any break-ins this year so far, but you never know," Devon said. "Do you want me to continue to take care of the place, or are you done with your business down in Hartley?"

"I'll have to head back to the city on Monday, so why don't you go home and take some time off while you can?"

"Thanks, Mr. Redhouse. If you need me, just call. I've already tended to the cattle, by the way. All that's left for today are the horses."

"Thanks, Devon. And, by the way, if you see that guy hanging around again, call the sheriff and let him ask the questions. Don't confront the guy yourself."

"Understood."

As the teenager left, Lori looked at Gene. "Do you think my stalker followed us here, or maybe checked out your place in case we showed up? So far he hasn't had any problem finding out where we're likely to go."

"True, but all we can do is speculate until we actually come across the guy." He remembered the two pickups he'd seen on the back roads, but neither had followed for long and they'd been the wrong color. "Either way, let's not assume we're out of harm's way. Keep an eye out. Right now I'm going to go do some chores like water the horses, put hay in the feeders and clean out stalls."

"I'll help out. That's basically what I did at the stables back in high school. Times may have changed, but horses haven't."

LORI WAS GLAD THAT IT WAS spring and that the days were finally getting longer. Although it was four in the afternoon the sun was still high enough in the sky to get the work done before dark.

As they brought down some bales of hay from the barn loft, they heard a horse's loud whinny.

"That's Grit," Gene said. "He's restless. I should try to work that edge off him on the lunge line before we settle him down for the night."

"Let me," she said.

He shook his head. "No, just take Ace out and put him in the corral. Once he's outside, it'll be easier for me to get Grit to follow."

"How will I know which is which?"

"Ace is a brown-and-white pinto, Grit is black-and-white, but don't worry. The easiest way to tell is to see which one comes up to you right away. That'll be Ace. The other horse, the one that'll probably try to bite if you get too close, that's Grit."

"Okay." Lori went into the barn and saw a pinto drinking water. "Hey, are you Ace?" she asked softly, trying to guess how dark he was. She couldn't see the other horse to compare.

The animal lifted his head, then turned around so that his hind legs faced her, ears pinned back. Guessing he wouldn't hesitate to kick if she stepped in there, she went to the next stall.

The other horse was one of the most beautiful animals she'd ever seen. As she drew closer, the horse nickered, a friendly greeting. As she continued speaking to him, trying to decide if he was white and black, or white and brown, his ears pricked forward as if not only listening, but interested.

"You must be Ace. Why don't you and I go outside," she said, reaching for the halter on a nearby hook, then going into the stall.

"It looks like it's you and me, guy." Lori fastened a halter on the horse, then tied a lead rope to the ring at the bottom and led him outside.

As she walked beside him, the horse seemed perfectly calm and content. Following her heart, she unfastened the rope and looped it through the bottom ring. Using the rope as makeshift reins, she jumped on the horse's back and rode him to the corral.

A second later Gene came out of the barn and stared at her. "*How* did you do that?"

"You told me to bring Ace out to the corral, so I didn't think you'd mind if I rode him around just a little. If you do, I can get off right now."

He shook his head.

Seeing Gene struggling with something, she added, "The other horse wouldn't even turn around for me. All he showed me were his hind legs, and I didn't want to risk getting kicked."

He nodded slowly. "Ace may have thought you were connected to Doc Linda Bailey. He hates our vet with a passion," he said. "The one you're riding—that's Grit."

She looked down at the gentle creature that was carrying her. "You're messing with me, aren't you?" she said with a half smile. "Well, it won't work."

She looked down at her mount, clicked her tongue, and the animal began to lope, taking easy, gentle strides.

Gene watched them in silence.

"Ace likes me," she said and smiled happily. This was heaven. It was her favorite gait. It felt as if you were on a giant rocking horse. "He moves so smoothly."

Five minutes later, she rode him over to where Gene stood, and slid to the ground. Even after she unfastened the halter, freeing the horse, it remained by her side.

"Grit doesn't accept riders easily. Consider yourself the chosen one."

"Are you serious?" she asked, giving him a long, hard look. "*This* is the problem horse you've been telling me about?"

"Yeah. You should hear some of Paul's stories." At the mention of the name, the horse snorted derisively.

She laughed. "He must be sending the wrong signals or it's a personality conflict. It happens." She patted Grit's neck, pulled his massive head closer to her and blew in his nostrils. The animal seemed to mellow out. "I hope you'll let me ride him again. He's really terrific."

"Sure. Anytime," he said. "You're used to riding bareback?"

"Yeah," she said and smiled. "When I worked at the stables, I often got the feeling that some people liked the way they looked on the horse more than they liked the horse itself. I wasn't interested in sitting pretty. I enjoyed the freedom of going bareback. I felt more in contact with the horse that way."

"You'll always have a standing invitation to come riding at Two Springs." He glanced back. "I better get Ace and turn him out. It's time to feed the other horses out in the pasture and top off their water, too, then I'll muck out the stalls."

"I'll take care of the stalls."

"Not necessary," he said. "You took care of Grit, and that was the hard part."

"Not for me," she said, laughing. "You've helped me a lot, so let me give you a hand with whatever needs doing."

"Balance," Gene said with a nod. "Let's get started."

Chapter Thirteen

By the time they'd tended the other horses and finished cleaning the stalls, it was dusk. Gene and Lori led Ace and Grit back into their stalls, where there was fresh hay waiting for them in their feeders.

"How come you keep these two in here instead of out in the pasture?"

"Grit needs to be around people, and he's also too hard to catch if he's not in an enclosure. Believe it or not, he's not always the gentleman you saw today. Ace is company for Grit. He's also normally the steadiest ride I've got, so I keep him here for Devon. He needs an available, steady mount to do things like check the fence line and get around the ranch. Ace doesn't spook easily and he'll tell you if danger's close by. When his ears go flat, you can figure that a snake or another predator is in the immediate area."

"You've got a good life here," she said, placing Grit inside his stall. "I envy you."

"I'm glad you see it that way. My brothers prefer to work in the city, but I wouldn't trade Two Springs for anything. I've got sixty-five acres, but that's only a fraction of the huge ranch Two Springs used to be back in the late eighteen hundreds. Still, for now, it's enough," he said. "I'm also hoping my spread will eventually become a place my brothers will learn to use as an escape from their high-pressure jobs."

"Yours has pressures, too," she said.

"Yeah, it does, but they're a different sort. The guys deal with lawlessness of one kind or another. Here I contend with nature, which has no agenda. It can be unpredictable, and the challenges—whether bad weather, drought or fires—can all test a man. But for the most part, hard work will determine my destiny."

She looked around, enjoying the sunset. "It's so beautiful here. I can see why you've chosen to call it home."

"Maybe you're meant to be a rancher, too."

She smiled. "I love animals and the outdoors, and if I could afford to buy a place like this, I'd go for it in a second. Not for ranching so much, but for raising horses. The time I worked at the stables was the happiest of my life."

He sat down on a bale of straw and began wiping off one of the bits with a damp cloth. "You do have a way with horses."

"No, not really. I get along with some, but not with others. Ace, for example, wanted to kick me through the side of the barn."

He laughed. "No, he's mostly all show and no

action. I just forgot how much he hates the vet visits, and Ace has a way of holding a grudge. Normally, he's not like that. Grit, too, wasn't acting like himself. You should see him around Paul. Grit goes out of his way to torment my brother."

"Maybe Grit noticed that I'm much prettier and sweeter smelling."

Gene roared with laughter. "I'm going to share that with Paul next time I see him."

Finished with the bits, Gene hung the bridles back up on a hook. Then, placing an arm over Lori's shoulder, he walked out of the barn with her, heading for the main house.

He remained quiet, thinking of *Hosteen* Silver's message. He'd said that as the unlikely happened, the lost one would show him the way. He'd just seen Grit accept a rider, and that was as unlikely as things got. As for the second part, Lori had been searching for direction in her life....

An explosive bang suddenly shattered his train of thought and he heard a bullet whine overhead, dangerously close.

Reacting in a heartbeat, Gene grabbed her hand and pulled her to the ground beside the pump shed. "Stay down!" he said, as he tried to spot the shooter.

"What do we do? He's armed and we aren't," she whispered. "And I don't even have my cell phone."

"Me neither, so our only chance is to work our way to the house. I've got my rifle in there and can even the odds. Once we're inside, stay away from the windows and doors and call the sheriff's department in Cortez. If the sniper tries to come in, lock yourself up in one of the rooms and stay flat on the floor. Let me deal with him."

Moving in a crouch, they worked their way to the corner of the shed, watching in every direction as they hugged the walls. There were no more shots. Now all they had to do was make a run for the back door—across about a hundred feet of open ground.

Lori took a quick glance around the corner of the pump house. "Maybe that's it. He took his best shot, missed, then decided to take off."

Gene shook his head, motioning for her to be silent. It was quiet for about a minute, then a pair of doves suddenly flew out from beneath a tree beside the house.

Someone was close. As Gene listened he heard muted footsteps.

"He knows our plans and is between us and the house now," Gene whispered. "Stay low and circle back around the pump house, then head for the barn. Use the pump house to screen your movements. We won't be able to reach the pickup or get to the house without giving him a clear shot, so we'll have to use the horses to get away. When we reach the barn I'll grab a bridle and get Ace out of his stall. We'll ride double and head for Crossroads Ranch. Devon and his dad will help us out."

They made it back to the barn double time. Gene got the bridle on Ace as Lori grabbed Grit's halter.

"Ace doesn't like me. Let me take Grit. It'll be faster than riding double," she said.

"Yeah, okay. Let's go," he whispered.

She led Grit out of his stall, but as she passed by Ace, the gelding slipped Gene's grip on the reins and spun, ready to kick.

"Ace, quit!" Gene grabbed the reins and gave them a quick tug, then took a second bridle from a hook. "Here, use this on Grit instead of the halter and rope. You'll have more control."

She made the change in seconds, then started to lead the horse out. Suddenly a dark figure blocked their way.

"That's far enough," the man ordered, pointing a Western-style revolver at Gene. The weapon fit the situation—the cowboy with the .44 wore a red bandanna over his face like an outlaw from an old Western. "The woman comes with me."

Gene, his hand still holding Ace's reins, moved closer. A few more steps and he'd make a move for the man's gun.

"I'm not after you, Redhouse," the man said. "Stop or I'll gun you down."

The man's voice sounded familiar to Gene, but he couldn't put a name to it. "Who sent you?" Gene demanded, hoping to stall.

"Don't know, don't care," the man spit out. "You, sweetie," he said, pointing the gun at Lori, who hadn't moved. "Let go of the reins and come with me if you ever want to see Redhouse again."

Lori was holding Grit tightly. He was prancing nervously, ears pinned back. "All right." She let go of Grit's reins, then took a step forward.

Grit, already spooked, snorted, ducked his head, then suddenly brushed past Lori at a gallop.

The gunman jumped back, but the horse caught his outstretched arm and spun him around, knocking him face-first into the barn door. Grit thundered past him out into the paddock, bucking like a wild mustang.

Their would-be kidnapper, who'd dropped his gun, spun around in a panic, trying to find his weapon.

Gene leaped forward, doubling the guy up with a punch in the gut. He followed with an uppercut to the chin that bounced the back of the man's head against the side of the barn with a hollow thud.

The man ducked his head and hurled himself at Gene, but Gene raised his foot and met his charge with a boot to the chest. The blow forced Gene backward, but his opponent was knocked to the ground, landing with his back against the wall.

Seeing that Lori had already retrieved the man's gun, Gene yanked the bandanna off their assailant's face.

Now he recognized the guy. Gene took a step away from the dazed man, who was rubbing the back of his head and cursing, his lips moist with blood.

"Well, if it isn't Duane Hays," Gene said. "I

thought they'd thrown you into the county jail after your last brawl."

Never taking his eyes off Hays, Gene took the offered revolver from Lori, then asked her to go to the house and call 911. While Lori took off, Gene remained with his prisoner.

"I want to know who hired you, Hays. Keep in mind that no one around here would say a word if I ended it right here for you. You came onto my property and started shooting, held us at gunpoint, then tried to kidnap the woman. I have a witness, and that's all the sheriff will need to know."

"I need to reach for my wallet so I can show you something," Hays said.

"Then do it slowly, Hays. If you make the wrong move, it'll be the last thing you do." For emphasis, Gene cocked the hammer with his thumb.

Duane moved carefully, his eyes on Gene. "Chill out, will you, and keep your finger away from that hair trigger. All I was doing was trying to make enough money to get me out of this rat hole of a county. After your neighbor fired my ass, I haven't been able to find work anywhere. Times have been tough. My trailer got repoed last week and I'm living out of my truck."

"You should have thought of all that before you showed up for work falling down drunk."

"Yeah, yeah, I hear you." He brought out his wallet and showed Gene one half of a hundred-dollar bill. "The guy told me I'd get the other half when

I delivered the woman. Without her I've got nothing."

"That's getting pretty desperate. What were you supposed to do with her?" Gene pressed.

"Deliver her, alive and well. That's it. He insisted that the deal was off if I hurt her."

"*Who* told you? You must have met the man if he gave you half the C-note."

"I was at the Crazy Horse Tavern over in Cortez. The bouncer threw me out on my butt when I came up five bucks short on my tab. That's when this dude came up to me."

"Who? And I won't repeat the question."

"Never met the guy before. Just a regular white guy—about five-ten, not thin, not fat, clean shaven. Had on a dark windbreaker and a ball cap."

"That doesn't tell me much," Gene growled.

"I'm not keeping anything from you. It was dark outside, I was wasted and that's all I can remember." He added, "He was a white-collar city dude, too, not a working man."

"How could you tell?"

"He gave me a hand up off the ground and his palm was soft, like a baby's."

"Okay, so where were you supposed to meet this accountant type after you had Lori?"

"I was told to call him by a certain time and he'd give me the details. He also told me not to be late calling, or he'd be long gone. He said he'd assume I fouled things up and skedaddle."

"What time did he give you?" Gene showed Duane his watch.

"Fifteen minutes ago," he said. "I picked up a nail and had to change a flat, then I had to wait till you two came outside. My bet is that he's in the next county by now. That guy was as jumpy as a toad in a hot skillet."

Gene started to press Hays for more information, but heard the wail of a police siren.

A second later Lori ran back into the barn. "There was an officer in the area, so the deputy's heading straight here. We'll need to let him in. Shall I go?"

Gene fished a key out of his pocket and handed it to her, then gestured for her to come closer. "The lock inside needs the code word *bear*," he whispered in her ear.

She smiled. "I'll be right back."

LORI SAT IN GENE'S LIVING room, waiting for the police to finish questioning him. Sheriff's deputies had already placed Duane Hays in the backseat of a patrol car and spoken to her.

The deputy who'd questioned Gene eventually came back into the room, and Gene followed seconds later. "Ms. Baker, we're taking the suspect to the station now. Our detectives will continue to question him there. If Hays knows who hired him, he'll probably make a plea deal and give us a name," the deputy said. "We'll be in touch."

"What about the phone number he was supposed to call?" Gene asked.

"We'll be checking that out, too, but it was probably a burn phone, a cheap, prepaid throwaway."

After all the deputies left, Lori sat on the couch with Gene. "So much for a few days in paradise."

He gave her surprised look. "Do you really see Two Springs that way?"

She smiled, sensing how much the possibility pleased him. "I can't imagine a better life than owning a place like this one. Sure, there's hard work, but it's the kind that satisfies you. Of course, I'd have to save up for decades before I could afford to buy a ranch even half this size."

"I hear you. I worked as a long-haul trucker for years just to get the down payment together. In those days I practically lived behind the wheel and slept at truck stops, but knowing what my goal was made it bearable."

"I'm hoping to take the next step up by restoring my house, then selling it at a profit. If the market ever picks up, that is."

"Take it one step at a time," he said, then stood. "We better get going. We can't stay here anymore. Whoever hired Hays obviously knows about my ranch. We'll have to find a place where backup's close by and where we can sleep without having one eye open."

"That would be great, but we've exhausted all the possibilities."

"No, not yet, we haven't. When I'm in a bind I can always count on my brothers to come through for me. I trust them and you can, too."

"Trust...that's never come easily to me. Does it to you?" she asked, meeting his gaze.

"No, I've seen too much of life."

"So you do understand why I hold back."

He paused, then nodded slowly. "You want to know that I won't break your heart somewhere along the way," he said. "But although I would do everything in my power not to hurt you, I can't promise that won't happen."

"I know," she said in a quiet voice. "If only we could just close our eyes, wish really hard and make all our dreams come true."

"Sometimes what we need to be happy is right in front of us. We just have to find the courage to claim it."

She felt herself drowning in that steady gaze. Before she could reach out to him, he stood and walked to the window.

"Get your things," he said. "We have to get moving before this guy realizes that his plan fell through and tries something else."

Chapter Fourteen

Car trips always made her sleepy and it was no different now in Gene's smooth-riding pickup. Somehow she'd drifted off and didn't wake up until they reached the outskirts of Hartley.

She opened her eyes with effort and looked around, trying to reorient herself. "Oh, jeez, I didn't mean to drift off again while you were driving. You should have woken me up!"

"You were exhausted, and I figured that since tomorrow's Sunday I'll catch some sleep once we get to Paul's."

"I never heard you call him."

"That's because I haven't—not yet anyway."

"It's late. Maybe he's asleep."

He shook his head. "Doubtful. Paul doesn't sleep much these days. After being involved in a shootout that left him wounded and his partner dead, Paul's changed, both inside and out. He's struggling with a lot of unresolved issues." He glanced at her and shook his head, preempting any questions. "I can't say more. One Navajo shouldn't speak for another."

They soon arrived at the coffee shop and Gene parked in the back.

He pulled his cell phone out of his pocket and got his brother on the second ring. Gene explained briefly that they needed a place to stay and, a moment later, placed the cell phone back into his pocket. "Okay, let's go."

They went upstairs and, by the time they reached the top floor, Paul opened the door.

Moments later they were inside Paul's small one-bedroom apartment. From what Lori could see, the living room furniture was comprised of a large wooden desk with several computers and monitors hung on the wall behind it. Adjacent to it, on a second desk, stood a printer and a small flat-screen TV set broadcasting the local news. A comfortable-looking sofa and chairs were wedged in between both desks.

"There's been nothing new on your case, but the good part is that the police department's work slowdown will be ending soon. The two groups are meeting again, and word is there's finally progress on the negotiations."

She took the leather chair Paul offered her. Gene straddled one of the two wooden ones around the second table, his arms resting on the back.

"We've got a problem," Gene said, updating Paul

on the events with Duane Hays and his secretive employer.

Paul remained in front of one of the computers, listening carefully. "Your suspect clearly has access to some extremely useful databases if he can find you that easily. He might be a Realtor." He looked at Lori. "Who did you deal with when you bought your house?"

"It was a direct sale by the owner. The house belonged to an elderly woman who held my current job at the DMV. I replaced her after she had a stroke," Lori said. "I'd heard that she wanted to sell the house, so I went to take a look at it. The place was falling apart, but the price was incredible, so I bought it immediately."

"You still had to deal with the loan and title people. The county clerk's office, too, I would imagine," Paul said. "The suspect could work at those locations, or any other business that has access to the same kinds of records. I think you need to work harder to put somebody else besides Harrington on that list of suspects."

"I'll keep trying, but in the meantime, isn't there a way we could stake out Bud's house? We know he's been there."

Paul shook his head. "The problem is that I'm working on a case, and Dan's doing a training op right now. You two can't do it because it'll put you in the line of fire. In other words, by trying to catch him, he may catch you—*if* he's the guy who's been causing all your problems."

"I can't just keep running. Sooner or later, he's going to catch up to me."

Paul looked at Gene. "She's got a point, but you've got a say in this, too."

"Lori, I think you're after the wrong man. I know that you *want* to believe it's Harrington. Better the devil you know than the one you don't. I understand all that, but don't let that close your eyes to other important facts. The man after you is clearly interested in something he thinks you have," Gene said. "Why else break into your house or try to steal your purse? That doesn't fit Harrington."

Paul leaned back and stared at an indeterminate spot across the room. "From what I've been able to uncover, Harrington's a small-time jewelry maker who specializes in modern silver jewelry, not Native American look-alikes. He works from home and sells mostly direct and wholesale. He also has a regular booth at the Second Street flea market. He's there every weekend."

"Tomorrow's Sunday," she said, looking at Gene. "Why don't we go to the flea market? He's not likely to give us a problem in the middle of a crowded place."

Gene considered it, then nodded. "I think that's a good idea."

"That means you two are going to need some sleep," Paul said. "I've got to wait up for an important email, so I'll be crashing on the couch. Why don't you two share my bed?" he said, then glanced at Lori. "Or feel free to tell Gene to grab a pillow and sleep on the floor."

She laughed. "We'll share and leave the door open, so feel free to come in whenever you want," she told Paul.

"The bedroom's down the hall. You can't miss it."

As she walked off, Paul pulled Gene back. "If I open the front door, the bedroom door will close on its own. You want me to give you thirty minutes or so, then make sure I create a draft?"

Gene laughed. "Not my style, bro, but thanks for the thought."

LORI WANTED TO SLEEP BUT soon realized that was impossible. She could feel the warmth of Gene's body beside hers on the bed, and images that could have set fire to the pages of the steamiest romance novel kept popping into her head.

After several minutes she heard Gene hiss out a breath. "This isn't going to work. I can't stop thinking about...you."

"Maybe we could just cuddle," she said.

He sat up and shook his head. "It wouldn't stop there."

"Yes, it would. We wouldn't have a choice. Your brother's less than twenty feet away."

"I'd nail the door shut and tell him to get earphones," he growled and stood.

As her gaze dropped, her mouth went dry. His jeans were bulging and he looked...well, huge. She sighed.

He gave a grin that was nothing less than pure masculine pride. "I'm going out there to join Paul."

"You haven't had any sleep, but I have. Take the bed. I'll keep your brother company."

He shook his head. "Thanks, but no. He and I need to talk. Among other things, I'd like to tell him about you and Grit."

She smiled. "You just want to bug him."

He grinned from ear to ear. "Hey, a man's got to have a little fun."

GENE CLOSED THE DOOR BEHIND him and went out to the living area. Paul was sitting atop the small sofa reading a software manual.

"For a slow-moving guy, that sure didn't take you long, did it?" Paul said with a sideways grin.

"We didn't—" He glowered at his brother, then glanced around. "You used to go camping. Don't you have a sleeping bag?"

"Yeah, but the zipper sticks."

"That's the story of your life," Gene said and ducked as Paul threw some balled-up socks at him.

"I have a foam pad you can use if you're feeling dainty," Paul said.

Gene chuckled. "I'm dainty, but you're the one keeping the couch?"

"Don't blame me if she ran your sorry butt out.

That would have *never* happened to me. I think you've been spending too much time sweet-talking horses. When was the last time you had a woman?"

"I don't keep score," he snapped. "Now where's the foam pad?"

"Closet."

As Gene unrolled the thin pad of resilient bedding, he glanced up at Paul. "You should have seen Lori with Grit. She walked right up, attached his halter without even a flinch, then, with only a rope through the halter ring, rode him bareback around the corral. No problem, no fuss, no biting threats, no flattened ears—nothing."

"That horse has good taste in women." Paul retrieved the email he'd been waiting for, then shut down the computer.

"Speaking of women, have you thought any more about the story *Hosteen* Silver left for us in his safe-deposit box, the one about Changing-Bear-Maiden?" Gene asked him. "There's a message there somewhere."

"I agree, but I haven't got any answers. The truth is I've had a problem remembering the original story well enough to look for discrepancies in the account he left behind for us."

"I can help you there," Gene said. "Here's a summary." He lapsed into a momentary silence, putting his thoughts together, then continued. "Changing-Bear-Woman was first a beautiful maiden who lived with her brothers. She turned down a lot of suitors, but then Coyote came courting. She knew he had a reputation as a trickster, so she decided to discourage him by offering a series of impossible challenges. If he overcame all of those, she promised she'd marry him."

"I remember now," Paul interjected. "Somehow, Coyote completed all those tasks and she was forced to marry him. But not long after that she was corrupted by her husband. She turned evil and learned how to change into a bear. From that point on, she ceased to be a mortal woman. By becoming Changing-Bear-Woman, her old self was completely destroyed."

"Exactly. And when Coyote became bored with married life, he dumped her. That really set her off. She went looking for him and killed everyone who got in her way, including her former family, all except her youngest brother, who hid from her," Gene said.

"The brother was forced to restore the balance by destroying what she'd become. However, he promised her that she'd live on in other forms and serve the *Diné*. A part of her body became the first piñon nut, another yucca fruit and so on," Gene said.

"Thanks for refreshing my memory. I can reread the original to fill in the details. What I do remember is how *Hosteen* Silver wanted us to learn from this story that good can be corrupted by evil, but conversely evil can be defeated with a lot of persistence and sacrifice," Paul said.

They both remained silent for a while. Finally Paul spoke. "*Hosteen* Silver liked challenging us. That's why he left us that story and, me, that damned horse."

Gene lay down and stared up at the ceiling. "Yeah, I think so, too, but I also think *Hosteen* Silver left Grit to you for a specific reason. It was more than just a way to test you."

"All I have to do is figure out what lesson he wanted me to learn."

"Hope you don't get trampled first."

"Good night, bro," Paul mumbled.

"Don't you mean shut up?"

Paul didn't reply. After a while, Gene turned his head and looked toward the bedroom door. Convinced he could hear Lori breathing, he slowly drifted off.

Chapter Fifteen

Lori stirred awake slowly, then glanced at the clock beside her on the nightstand. As she saw the time, she drew in a sharp breath and jumped out of bed. It was ten in the morning!

Lori cleaned up quickly, then went into the living area and joined the men.

Gene gave her a wide smile as she came in. "About time you woke up."

"Sorry! I never thought I'd oversleep like that or I'd have asked you to wake me up," she said. "So how about letting me make it up to you guys? I'll buy breakfast downstairs—providing it doesn't go over twenty bucks and they serve breakfast."

Paul laughed. "Does she always set limits like that?"

"Yeah, 'fraid so," Gene said. Looking back at Lori, he chuckled. "I'll go down and pick up something for us, then after breakfast we'll get going."

Paul glanced over at them. "Are you two still planning to make a run to the flea market?"

"Yeah," Gene said. "Maybe we can catch up to

Harrington. I think it's about time he and I had a little talk."

"Put your feelings aside," Paul said. "Without a clear head, your enemy will have the advantage."

"I hear you," Gene said, standing. "Burritos, everyone?" Seeing them nod, he headed to the door. "I'll be back in a few minutes."

"Coffee, too?" she asked as he reached for the handle.

"No need," Paul said. "I was just about to make a full pot."

After Gene left, Paul quickly started the coffee brewing, then sat back down in front of his computer keyboard.

"You're worried about Gene and Bud meeting up at the flea market, aren't you? But why? Gene isn't the kind of man who acts out of anger," she said. "Even under fire, he thinks, then acts."

"What you've said describes Gene at least three-quarters of the time, if not more. It takes a lot to get him riled up, but once that happens, all hell breaks loose."

She gave him an incredulous look.

"Really," Paul insisted. "Let me tell you about one incident that still sticks in my mind, though it was years ago. One weekend after Preston and I went to live with *Hosteen* Silver, Gene came to visit. While he was there talking to Preston and me, three Anglo men came to the door, looking for trouble. *Hosteen* Silver had treated a Navajo woman who happened to be married to one of the Anglos. The husband viewed the Navajo way as an affront to his religion and had come with two buddies to teach our foster father a lesson.

"They pushed their way into the house and tried to grab *Hosteen* Silver. Gene was standing beside him, and before Preston and I could even cross the room, Gene took all of them on. He punched the lead man in the gut, doubling him over, then kicked the second guy in the chest, knocking him into the third guy and tossing both back out onto the porch. I saw him pick up the one he'd punched as if he weighed no more than a sack of feed, and throw him on top of the other two, who were scrambling to their feet. By the time Preston and I reached the door, it was all over. The men ran back to their truck and we never saw them again," Paul said. "When you push him far enough, Gene can be like a bear on a rampage."

"I can't even imagine Gene doing that," she said.

"He did," Paul said somberly.

She thought of how he'd taken on that cowboy, Duane, who'd shot at them at Two Springs Ranch. He'd done only what was necessary and had remained in control of himself all the way. He'd pulled back immediately when the man had stopped fighting.

"You see a slow-talking, laid-back rancher and he's just that most of the time, but don't let that fool you. There's more to any bear than what you see at a glance."

She was about to ask him more when Gene walked in. "The parking lot's full and business is booming, but I couldn't see anyone watching the place."

They ate breakfast quickly. Paul had an appointment with a new client and needed time to prepare.

"Business is good?" she asked Paul, who kept looking over at his computer monitor.

"Yeah, it is. I never expected to be this busy. When I opened the agency I just saw it as a way to redirect my focus and move in a new direction."

"You've been through a lot," she said softly, gesturing to his shoulder.

"Yeah, you might say that, but I can't just sit in an easy chair and watch surveillance monitors until my shoulder heals—if it ever does."

"Are you still in pain?" she asked in a gentle voice.

"Sometimes," he said, not answering her directly. "That's why I decided to try a remedy *Hosteen* Silver used to recommend to his patients. So far it's been working."

"What are you using?" Gene asked. *"Tsinyaachéch'il?"*

"Yeah."

"What is that?" Lori asked.

"Creeping barberry, or Oregon grape. It grows in the high country." Gene looked back at his brother.

"That might also explain the success of your new business."

"I don't follow you, bro," Paul said.

"That plant is also said to remove bad luck. Remember when I flunked two physics tests in a row? He made up a special medicine pouch using *Tsinyaachéch'il* for me."

"Did it work?" Lori asked, unable to suppress her curiosity.

"I got a C on the next physics test, which is as high as I ever got in that subject," Gene said.

"Maybe I should start carrying some of that," Lori said. "We could sure use some good luck."

Paul smiled. "I'll add some to my brother's medicine pouch." He glanced at Gene and added, "You still carry one, don't you?"

Gene reached into his pocket and brought out a small leather bag. "Of course I do. I keep the bear fetish he gave me inside it, too."

"What exactly is a medicine pouch?" she asked.

"It contains ritual items like sacred pollen and other collected substances. It's meant to attract good and repel evil," Gene said. "*Hosteen* Silver made one for each of us to carry."

"It sounds like a very good thing to have," she said.

"I could make one for you if you'd like," Paul said.

"I'd love to have one. Thank you very much," she

said, then looked at Gene. "That's okay with you, isn't it?"

"Of course. I would have offered to make one for you myself if I'd known you were interested."

Paul joined them about ten minutes later carrying a small leather pouch. "There's some creeping barberry inside, some sacred pollen and a small rock crystal."

"Does each mean something special, or is it the combination that's most important?" she asked.

"Both," Paul said. "According to Navajo teachings at the time of the beginning, a rock crystal was placed in the mouth of each person so words would have power. Pollen is the symbol of light and well-being. When placed together, their powerful medicine is said to make wishes spoken aloud come true."

She took it from his hands, handling it carefully and with respect. "What a beautiful gift. I don't know how to thank you."

"You just did," Paul said. "There's one more thing I would have liked to put in there. The hearts of our medicine pouches are the fetishes they contain." He glanced at Gene. "Lynx is my spiritual brother, Bear is yours. What should hers be?"

"I'm not sure. It's a match that'll take some thought. Leave that to me," Gene said.

After breakfast, Gene and Lori got ready to leave. Saying goodbye, Lori impulsively hugged Paul and, as she did, felt him stiffen.

"Did I hurt you?" she said, immediately mortified.

He shook his head.

Gene laughed. "My brother's not big on shows of affection—ones that don't include fists, that is."

Once she and Gene were on their way, Lori brought the medicine pouch out from her purse and held it in the hollow of her palm. "This is such a special gift."

"Yes, it is."

"Do you believe in its powers?" she asked.

"Traditionalists do," he said after several beats, "but I'm a Modernist. I look at the bundle as a way of showing respect for ritual knowledge. It's an affirmation that there's a lot more to our world than what the eye can see," he said. "It honors the unseen gifts."

As she considered what he'd said, Lori thought of how that also applied to the attraction between Gene and her. Instead of fear, maybe she should be grateful for the gift life had brought her and stop weighing down her feelings for Gene with expectations and fear.

"We're here," Gene said, bringing her out of her musings.

She glanced around, suddenly aware they'd arrived at the site of the weekly flea market, a section of the fairgrounds enclosed with a high chain-link fence. "It's time to go hunting," she said, bracing herself.

"Wrong mind-set," he said, shaking his head. "You'll have to relax and play the role of Sunday shopper. The best tactic is to blend in and just talk to people. I have one of Paul's company IDs so I can pass myself off as an investigator if necessary, but a low-key approach is best. We have no legal standing, so when we find Harrington, we'll have to persuade him that it's to his advantage to deal directly with us to solve the problem."

As they walked to the entrance, Lori fell into step beside him. Soon they reached the long rows of booths, and she pointed to one in particular about twenty yards away. "They have some jewelry there and though it's not the same type Bud sells, the vendor may know Bud by reputation."

They approached the booth and Lori glanced down at the colorful beaded jewelry. "I was looking for silver necklaces," she said. "By any chance do you know a man by the name of Bud Harrington? I've heard he specializes in modern designs."

The vendor, a sunburned woman in her fifties with stringy blond hair, made a face of disgust. "He's here—somewhere. Frankly I don't get what the fuss is about. His stuff is generic crap."

"'Fuss?' What do you mean?" Gene asked immediately.

"You're the second person who has asked about him in the past five minutes."

"That's interesting. Who was the first?" Gene pressed.

"I don't know the guy. He was about six foot two or three, black hair, dark eyes," she said. "Bud's usually not far from my booth—we play off each other—but I haven't seen him around today. He may have traded locations with another regular." Looking around, the blonde woman added, "That's the guy who was asking about him—" she pointed "—the one with the greasy black hair."

Gene saw the man, who was wearing jeans and a tan corduroy jacket, end his conversation with another vendor, then move down the line of booths.

"Let's go," he said to Lori.

"Wait a second." Lori glanced back at the woman. "What did that other man want with Harrington?"

The lady shrugged. "No idea, but he sure looked pissed."

Lori thanked her, then, as they hurried down past a half-dozen booths, the man in the corduroy jacket turned the corner.

"Hurry before we lose him," Lori said, striding more quickly now.

Gene pulled her back. "Don't rush. If he's involved with Harrington, we might just catch both of them if we hang back a little. If you hurry along you'll stand out even more and he's bound to notice a beautiful woman. Stroll, like we're here just looking around. Then we'll approach him casually and start a conversation."

"If I'm right and Harrington's involved in whatever's going on, the second *he* sees me..." she said, letting her words trail off.

"That's why I want to keep an eye on this guy and keep our distance. If Harrington doesn't surface soon, we'll go talk to mister greasy hair. We've heard he's pissed off at Bud, so he may see us as allies—'my enemy's enemy is my friend' type of thinking."

They closed in as the man stopped at a booth that sold paintings and other decorative art. Feigning an interest in the paintings, Gene and Lori listened as he spoke to the woman behind the counter. After a moment the man reached into his jacket pocket and brought out a big plastic bag, which he laid on the crude tabletop.

"You clearly love fine silver," he said, pointing to the multistrand liquid silver necklace she wore. "The pieces I have here were made especially for a shop near Santa Fe's Indian Market, but the place closed before they could be delivered. The entire set was crafted by Bud Harrington—a local silversmith. You can see Mr. Harrington's mark here on the reverse side of the blossom."

The woman looked at the piece carefully. "There's a green hint in some of the crevices. This is silver plate. I'll pass."

Gene stepped up and, following his instincts, decided to flash the ID Paul had given him. "I'd like to talk business with you, sir. Why don't we go find someplace more private?" Gene placed his hand on the man's shoulder.

Startled, the man stepped back so quickly he collided with Lori. Spinning around, he shoved her into Gene, then raced away, dodging around members of the crowd with the agility of a buck in the forest.

"Wait here," Gene said, then took off after the guy.

The running man reached the end of the row, then suddenly cut left and disappeared. By the time Gene reached the corner, the guy had vanished.

Gene stood there for a moment, watching the gathered crowd. The man at the booth two spaces down was talking to an elderly couple shopping for bread. The vendor advertised a variety of fresh rolls, bread and cakes.

Sitting on a bench at the back of the booth was a small sheltie. As Gene looked over, he saw that the dog was watching him.

Gene looked around, then back at the dog, communicating without words and watching the animal for response.

The dog turned his head to the left and lowered his muzzle, staring at something behind Gene. Following its gaze, Gene saw the big white blood-services trailer, a fixture at events like this. Puzzled, he looked back at the sheltie. The dog continued looking at the same spot.

Gene crouched down and, looking beneath the

trailer, spotted a pair of jean-clad legs. He recognized the shoes.

Gene nodded to the dog in silent acknowledgment and saw him lie down to watch.

Moving around so he could see both ends of the trailer, Gene waited a minute or two, then saw the guy stride out casually from behind the trailer.

The man entered a row of booths, then glanced over his shoulder. Spotting Gene, he instantly took off again, cutting between two booths and knocking over a trash can. He leaped up, then ran off, disappearing again around a booth.

Gene decided it was pointless to keep after the guy when there was another more effective solution. Unless the guy was Spider-Man, the only way he'd be able to get out was at the controlled entrance—the gate. It was time to wait for the guy in the jacket to come after him, not the other way around.

Gene reached the entrance a short time later, then stepped back behind a big concrete sculpture of a bear and waited.

Within thirty seconds, the man appeared, striding quickly toward the exit and looking over his shoulder. A private security guard in a gray uniform was also closing in, Lori at his side.

"That's the man," Lori said, pointing.

Gene stepped out, cutting the guy off. "Make this easy on yourself. All I want to do is talk."

The man looked over his shoulder at the burly security guard, then back at Gene. "What do you want from me?"

Lori caught up a second later. "Thanks for your help, sir," she told the security guard. "This jewelry belongs to the gentleman, but he didn't realize that he'd left it behind on the booth counter. My friend ran after him, but I guess he got the wrong idea."

Lori held out the bag with the silver-plated jewelry, and the man took it.

Gene, standing behind the guy, whispered, "If you don't cooperate, slick, she'll mention you were trying to pass this cheap stuff off as real."

The man looked at the security guard and smiled. "Thanks for going to all this trouble." As the security guard walked away, he glared at Gene and Lori. "You're a P.I. Why are you bugging me, and what the hell do you want?"

"Easy. We're not out to bust you for selling fake silver jewelry. We're looking for Bud Harrington," Lori said.

"Welcome to the club," he snapped. "That sleazeball sold me this fake crap. I've been trying to find him for two weeks now. I know he works out of his home, but he hasn't been there and he's been ducking my calls."

"So what's your name, pal?" Gene said, finally taking his hand off the man's shoulder in a gesture of cooperation.

"Denis Sosa." The man brought out a business card from his shirt pocket and handed it to Gene. "I buy jewelry here at the flea market and at yard sales, then sell the merchandise on the internet. But I don't deal in junk. Did Harrington rip you off, too?"

"Something like that," Gene answered. "If you see or hear from him or get any leads, give me a call." He pulled one of Paul's business cards from his wallet and wrote down his cell number on the back.

"Sure, but if I catch him first you'll have to visit him at the hospital." Sosa jammed the bag of jewelry back into his pocket, then strode back into the Sunday bazaar and disappeared into the crowd.

"Now what?" Lori asked Gene.

"I'm going to check him out. After that, we'll sit down and figure out our next step."

Chapter Sixteen

Once they were back in the truck Gene called Paul, but found out his brother was still with his client. He called Daniel next and was about to leave a message for him when he picked up.

"I know your Sundays are family time these days, but I need a favor. Can you run a quick background check for me?" Gene said, then gave him Sosa's name.

A few minutes later Daniel put the name through his computer. "Small-time merchant of odds and ends, suspected of fencing stolen merchandise. He's careful, though. He's been arrested twice but beat the rap both times due to lack of evidence."

"Thanks," Gene said. "I appreciate it. Now I know why he took off when he thought I was an investigator."

"I heard from Paul that you're still scrambling to get the guy who's after your lady."

Gene smiled. *His* lady. He sure liked the sound of that. "Something like that, yeah."

"Sounds to me like Bear's found a mate."

He started to deny it, but never got the chance.

"I better get going. I promised Holly I'd help her check out new home listings on the computer today, but before I go, there's something you need to know. Preston called Sergeant Chavez from Quantico and asked if he'd go speak to Harrington again. That was a no go, but Chavez sent a cruiser by his residence about thirty minutes ago just to check things out, and it looks like Harrington was there. I just got the word a few minutes ago and was about to call and let you know."

"Thanks. I'll head over there."

"Let me know if you need me," Daniel said, then hung up.

"Where are we going?" Lori asked as he got the truck started.

He told her what Daniel had said. "I want to drive by Harrington's place and see what's up."

They reached Harrington's home sometime later and, as they drove past it, they could see the mailbox was empty, and it looked like the pickup had been moved recently.

Gene circled, then parked by the curb one house down. "Wait here," he said. "I'm going to walk over and knock on his front door."

Lori reached for her door handle. "I'm going with you."

"No. Let me confront him. I want you to stand by with your cell phone in case things get ugly," Gene said, then walked off.

As Lori opened the door, he turned and shook his head. "Wait. That's the best backup you can give me."

With a nod, she stayed where she was. Lori watched as Gene walked to Harrington's home, then crossed over to the porch and knocked. After several moments he turned around and walked back to the pickup.

"What's going on?" she asked as he climbed in.

"No one's there now."

"How can you be sure?"

"I listened for sounds and looked for any play of light inside, but there was nothing," he said. "If he came by, he's already gone. The only way to be one hundred percent sure of that is for me to break in, but that might land us both in jail."

"Let's pass on that."

Soon afterward they left the neighborhood and Lori fell into a long silence.

"What's wrong?" he asked.

"I have to go to work tomorrow, but I'm no longer so convinced that I'm not posing a danger to the people there. Trouble seems to find me when I least expect it."

"I don't think you have anything to worry about at the DMV," Gene said, "but it won't hurt to take a few added precautions."

"Like what?"

"Your hair is a beautiful and distinctive color," he said, admiring that mass of honey-brown hair that cascaded around her shoulders. "Maybe a short, dark wig, along with clothes that look more... matronly."

"No bright colors, huh?" she said, looking down at her royal-blue blouse. She'd always loved jewel tones.

"Pick gray or white, something loose, too, that doesn't call attention to you."

"Doesn't sound like anything in my closet. I don't do bland, so I assume we're going shopping, then?"

He considered it. Remaining among crowds offered its own level of protection, but he had an even better idea, one that would guarantee their safety for at least a few hours.

"I don't want to go by your house if we can avoid it. We've been followed too much as it is. But I've got an idea. You're about the same size as my brother's wife, who wears more conservative clothing. I'm going to take you over to Dan's place. You can borrow something from her."

"Some women don't like loaning their clothes."

"If Holly objects, then we'll think of something else."

A short time later they arrived at the small, rectangular one-story warehouse. The metal structure was enclosed by a tall chain-link fence. Gene stopped at the gate, punched in a code on the lock, and the gate swung open.

"This is where he works?"

"And lives. They're in the process of finding a

home, but so far they haven't seen anything that's right for them."

A moment later the warehouse door opened and Dan stepped outside, a lovely auburn-haired woman by his side.

As Lori looked at the other woman's proportions, she knew Gene had been right. Though she wasn't as curvy as Daniel's wife, they probably wore the same size.

Gene made the introductions and Holly instantly gave her a hug. "I've been hearing all about your adventures from Paul. You must have been so scared!" she said, leading Lori inside and toward the kitchen area.

"Yes, but I'm also angry, which helps push back the fear a little," she said.

"I just made some fresh cinnamon rolls and brewed some coffee. Let's eat and talk. You can tell me all about it."

AS THE WOMEN DISAPPEARED behind the partition that separated the kitchen from the rest of the small warehouse facility, Daniel gave Gene a long look. "Preston heard what you've been up to from Paul and told me to tell you to bail—now."

Gene shook his head. "That's not going to happen."

"You've got it bad, don't you?"

"Shut up and listen," Gene growled.

Daniel forced himself to look serious, but a hint

of a smile still tugged at the corners of his mouth. "I'm here to help, bro. What do you need?"

Gene updated him. "I have to find a way to stop whoever's behind these attacks on Lori, but I'm out of ideas."

Dan exhaled in a hiss. "You're out of your element, country boy. This isn't your kind of fight."

"I'm fighting it anyway."

"She's not for you, bro. You need to rethink your involvement."

"What the hell are you talking about?"

"This one's not safe and predictable. She's a live wire and a visual distraction if there ever was one. That's gonna drive a guy like you nuts."

Gene's stare was glacial.

Dan grinned. "Here's my point. Where do you expect this all to lead, and are you sure she's thinking along the same lines?"

"I'm not planning that far ahead," he answered.

"Yeah, you are, 'cause that's the way you're wired," Daniel said. "You're in for a world of hurt, bro. She needs you now and she'll be grateful later, but that's not going to be enough for you, is it?"

He knew the truth when he heard it, but it was too late.

"Once this is over she might just go back to her life. Then where will that leave you? Have you thought all that out?"

"She'll make her own choices."

Before Daniel could answer, Lori came out looking much more conservative but absolutely gorgeous wearing Holly's navy slacks and silk blouse.

"I know you wanted plain, but the ruffles around the V-neck make it look less austere," Holly said.

"What do you think?" Lori asked Gene.

Dan looked at his brother, then bit back a grin.

"You look...beautiful and very classy," Gene said in a strangled voice. "But we still need to do something with your hair. Do you have a wig, Holly?"

"Wig? I don't use—"

"You've got one," Daniel said, interrupting her. "Remember the one you bought last Halloween for the mayor's special banquet? You decided to go as that reality show airhead. The heiress who's famous for being famous."

She smiled. "It was for a Health and Family Services fundraiser, and it was an easy costume." She looked back at Lori and shrugged. "I'd always wondered how I'd look as a blonde."

"Easy answer—you looked *hot*," Daniel said.

"Not quite. I looked like a mutant," she said and laughed. "Let me get it out and you can try it on. You've got very light brown hair, so it may not look as horrible on you as it did on me."

"Just how blond are we talking about?" Lori asked.

"Very. Think platinum. It'll give you a completely different look," Holly said.

"Try it," Gene said.

Lori returned several minutes later, followed

by Holly, and as Gene saw her, he sucked in his breath. He usually hated short hair on women, but she looked amazing.

Gene couldn't take his eyes off Lori. "No one will recognize you," he said, swallowing to aid the dryness in his throat. "But you need to wear something less...attention gathering."

"Okay, back to the drawing board," Holly said, leading Lori back to the bedroom. "Let's see if I've got any clothes that will make you look totally frumpy."

"Now I understand how she got under your skin," Dan said quietly as the two women disappeared.

Gene pinned him with a lethal glare. "Careful."

"Hey, just saying," Dan replied, stepping back and holding up his palms in mock surrender.

"Hey, guys, what do you think?" Lori said, coming back out several minutes later.

The wig was the same, but this time she was wearing black slacks, a pale blue T-shirt and a black jacket that hid her curves.

"Okay, that's better," Gene said. He could live with the austere business look. "You're still gorgeous, that'll never change, but dressed like this you're not quite so..."

"I'd watch your next word, buddy," Dan whispered from behind him.

"Yes?" Lori asked, waiting.

"Openly tempting?" Gene offered.

"Oh, thanks, I think," Lori said. "There was a compliment in there, right?"

"Absolutely," Gene said, then glanced back at Dan. "Now that we have this part settled, how about helping me do a much more thorough background check on Harrington?"

"Fine with me," Dan said. "Let's leave the ladies and you and I can do some serious digging."

"I'd like to help," Lori said.

Daniel shook his head. "Bad idea. I'm going to be calling in favors and accessing some confidential databases that you really don't need to know about. The fewer people involved, the better."

As Gene and Dan stepped around the partition to where the computers were, Dan gave Gene a hard look.

"I want to do a full background on Lori, too. Objections?"

"Why do you think that's necessary?" Gene shot back.

"Because the answer may be there."

"You think she's holding out on me?" Gene asked.

Dan shook his head. "Not necessarily. What worries me more is that you may both be missing something important because you're too close to the case. Just because it may seem inconsequential to her, or you, doesn't mean it's not the answer to all that's been going on. Sometimes, the more vested you are in a case, the less effective you are as an investigator. Too many preconceptions."

Gene nodded. "Yeah, you're probably right. Go ahead."

Daniel sat down in front of the computer on the left, then typed in two encrypted passwords. A new screen came up. "Okay, here we go."

EVENING TURNED INTO NIGHT, and after a brief dinner, Dan and Gene went to the computer again.

Back in the living area, Holly offered Lori a seat. "I've seen that fixed look on Daniel's face before. Did you see how he was at dinner? I asked him if he wanted more mashed potatoes, and he only heard me the third time. I could have served moist sand instead of potatoes and I don't think he would have noticed the difference."

Lori laughed. "They were both that way."

"That means it'll be an all-nighter for them. The brothers are always helping each other out. When Daniel and I had some problems not long ago, Gene was there for us one hundred percent. They'll take catnaps and probably have at least two full pots of coffee before sunrise. You and I will need our sleep, though, so I'm going to get you set up in the study. The couch there converts into a full-size bed. It's not fancy, but it's comfortable, and you'll be able to get some rest."

"I appreciate you going to all this trouble," Lori said, following her to the study.

"Gene's hooked on you," she said. "I'm glad to see it, too. I know Daniel worried that Gene would never really connect with anyone, outside of his brothers, that is."

"They're a very close-knit family, aren't they?" Lori commented, helping pull out and make the bed.

"Oh, yeah. The guys are there for each other no matter what. I've never met a family quite like theirs. I think they're even closer because they all went through hard times before going to live with *Hosteen* Silver."

"So far, I've only met Paul and Dan, but they're all good men."

"And capable of amazing loyalty," Holly said in a quiet voice. "They're as different as can be from one another, but their ties were forged by choice, and I think that's what makes them so strong."

"Whenever Gene talks about his foster father," Lori said, "he is always deeply respectful."

"I never had the chance to meet him myself, but from everything I've heard, he was one in a million."

They suddenly heard a loud crash, followed by raucous laughter.

Holly rolled her eyes. "There they go again."

"Go where?"

Holly stepped out into the hall and waved toward Daniel's office area. "That's how they'll stay awake and alert tonight."

Lori came out and caught a glimpse of the men wrestling on the floor, well away from the computers. Daniel pinned Gene to the floor, but in a flash, Gene twisted and pinned Daniel.

"You're still soft, city boy," Gene said, chuckling.

"You cheated! I can't fight you when you get me laughing like that," Daniel said.

"Yeah, well, I also won. You get to fix breakfast for all of us tomorrow."

They rose to their feet, Gene helping Daniel up, then they went to pick up the pieces of a ceramic mug.

"I really should buy metal cups," Holly said, shaking her head. "Whenever these guys get together, the roughhousing starts up in a hurry."

Lori smiled. "But they're the best of friends."

"Yeah, that they are. Before I met Daniel, I often wondered what it would have been like to grow up as part of a large family. Now I'm in one." She smiled at Lori.

"You two love each other very much, and I hear you're house hunting. You've a wonderful life together," Lori said with a touch of envy.

Holly smiled. "I've seen the way you and Gene look at each other. There's something very special going on between you guys, too."

"It's so...intense. Sometimes those feelings terrify me." Lori dropped her voice to a whisper. "But I'm also afraid I'll never feel this way again if we end up going our separate ways."

"Don't try looking so far into the future. If you do, you'll miss today."

"That's good advice." As Holly walked out of the room, Lori looked at Holly's blue fluffy slippers and sighed.

Sometimes when she had time to think, like now, she found herself missing silly things, like having some apple chamomile tea before bedtime, or padding around in her favorite hot-pink fluffy slippers. Yet, above and beyond all that lay the lingering fear of what she stood to lose once she regained them.

Chapter Seventeen

Gene and Lori left the next morning at eight in Daniel's sedan, just in case someone was watching for Gene's truck.

Lori had slept soundly, but she knew that Gene and Dan had been up most of the night, if not all. "You didn't get much sleep," she said, shifting the weight of her laptop tote so she could face Gene more squarely.

"No, but my time with Dan was well spent."

She heard the slight change in his voice and sat up even straighter. "You found out something really important, didn't you? I can hear it in your voice. What was it?"

Gene paused before he answered. "I don't know if this is good news or bad. Bud Harrington isn't our guy. He never has been."

"What? How can you be so sure?"

Gene pointed to the glove compartment. "There's a printout in there of the newspaper article Dan found. Check it out."

Lori reached for what appeared to be a section

taken from the *Hartley Messenger*'s society column, and read quickly, noting that it was dated yesterday. "I never knew about this! Bud got married last week in Las Vegas to Melinda Vaughn. She's the widow of Joseph Vaughn, the CEO of Hartley Mechanics— the oil services corporation. Melinda's one of the wealthiest women in the state."

"She's also at least twenty years older than Harrington. That's Harrington in the photo, right?" Gene asked.

"That's Bud." Then, as Lori read further, it hit her. "They didn't return to town until the day I called him. His phone was probably forwarded to her home, that place on the hill above the golf course. Now it makes sense. He's been staying with her, not on Pine Street."

"It also means he wasn't the man after you," Gene said. "Dan checked the flight manifest of the local airline and the hotel records, and the story checks out. Bud and the former Mrs. Vaughn were in Vegas getting married when this all started."

"No wonder Bud countered my accusation so quickly. He was afraid I'd screw up his sweet deal— marriage to a rich widow." She bit her bottom lip, not knowing whether to laugh or cry. "But where does that leave us?"

"I like the way you said 'us,' because I'm not going anywhere till we solve this and the man after you is behind bars."

Stunned, she leaned back in her seat. All her life

she'd encouraged people to think she was a free spirit, hiding the truth even from herself. Yet, the truth was that she wasn't 'free'; she was just afraid of getting hurt. Having no expectations, she couldn't possibly be disappointed by anyone or anything.

Now she was at a crossroads. If she surrendered her heart and things went wrong, she wasn't sure she'd ever be able to put the pieces together again. Yet not taking a chance also would exact its own share of pain and, worse—a lifetime of what-ifs.

"Today at work, try hard to remember any incident that could have made someone angry enough to come after you," he said, interrupting her thoughts. "Will you do that?"

"Yes, of course," she said.

As he pulled into the DMV's parking lot, he saw it was already crowded. "Go in through the front like a customer. Don't use the employee entrance."

"Got it."

Gene parked and watched her get out. "I've got your back. If there's trouble, I'm only a phone call away."

Gene waited until she walked inside the building, then drove off. Had the choice been his to make, he wouldn't have let her out of his sight today. Learning that Harrington couldn't have been the man stalking her had left him with a bad feeling.

He brushed those nagging thoughts aside. It was probably partly due to lack of sleep. All-nighters were harder on him these days than they'd been at one time.

Needing a jolt of caffeine, he stopped at the Chrome Dipstick, his favorite truck stop diner, and went inside. He'd have some of their world-class coffee in the big white mugs and maybe a sliver of their pecan pie, his favorite. If that didn't reenergize him, nothing would.

Gene went straight to the counter, which was topped with plate glass over a collection of old license plates from every state and some Canadian provinces. A second or two after he sat down, a familiar face came out from behind the café's double doors leading into the kitchen. Mrs. Nez was an elderly Navajo, a long-haul trucker's widow who'd worked here as far back as he could remember.

"I see you're still hard at work, Irene," Gene said, greeting her.

"Keeps the engine running," she said with an easy smile. "Now what can I get you, young man? The usual?"

He nodded. "I need some pecan pie and a mug of black coffee."

"Leaded or unleaded?" she asked.

"Make mine leaded. I need to keep my eyes open."

"Coming right up."

She returned moments later with the pie and coffee. "I'm glad you came by, Gene. I've been wanting to tell you how sorry I was to hear about your foster father. His absence will be felt, and not just by the *Diné*." He noted how she'd avoided saying his name, a custom among Navajos who didn't want to call the *chindi*. Belief in the *chindi*, the evil side of a man that was forced to remain earthbound while the good merged with the universe, was strong even among Modernists. "We all miss him."

"It's just too bad that he never took on an apprentice. That Navajo widow sure had her sights set on becoming a medicine woman, but I guess he turned her down."

"Huh?" Mrs. Nez gave him a surprised look. "I thought you boys knew about that. Rita something was her name, and she was crazy about your foster dad. I guess he didn't feel the same way about her," she said. "Maybe he never got over his wife."

Gene knew about *Hosteen* Silver's wife, though she'd passed away a few years prior to their arrival. Their foster father had seldom spoken about her, but it was clear that he'd loved her deeply. He and Dan had speculated that part of the reason *Hosteen* Silver had invited all of them into his life was to fill the void her death had created.

As Mrs. Nez moved away, he finished eating. The coffee had stirred him into alertness. As he thought of *Hosteen* Silver, Gene realized that there was still much they'd never known about him. Their foster father's focus had always been on who they could become, not on who they'd been, and with that in mind, he'd also not spoken of his own past.

Gene remembered the questions Daniel had raised about their foster father's death. Perhaps there was more to *Hosteen* Silver's story than they'd ever realized. Then again, the same could have been said for just about everyone, including Lori. People's lives were seldom as simple as they appeared to be on the surface.

As he thought about Lori, he smiled. Funny how his thoughts always returned to her. The connection between them seemed to grow stronger with each passing day. Then again, maybe the intensity of the chase was scrambling his brains, and once that highly charged situation was resolved, their feelings for each other would dissipate like morning fog under the sun.

Leaving a large tip for Mrs. Nez, he headed back out to the parking lot.

As he drove through town, he passed a familiar place. The Zuni man who'd carved fetishes for him and all his brothers had his shop here in Hartley. Gene turned, circled the block, then parked at the curb in front of the store.

Pablo Ortiz, a small, rotund man with gray hair and smiling eyes, greeted him from behind the old oak-and-glass counter, a relic itself probably a hundred years old. Gene said hello, then hung back as Pablo finished waiting on another customer. Passing the time, Gene searched beneath the glass, studying the stone fetishes resting on a rich velveteen cloth.

"It's good to see you, Gene," Pablo said at last, coming to join him. "So what can I do for you today? I saw you looking at my hand-carved fetishes. Did one catch your eye?"

"I'm trying to choose the right one to give a good friend," he said, "and that's turning out to be tougher than I'd thought. She's a complicated person."

"Tell me a bit more about her."

Gene paused, considering his words carefully. The right match was essential. "She's a woman of courage, but the past weighs her down, and those shadows keep her dreams shackled to the ground."

Pablo considered it for a long time, and Gene didn't interrupt him.

"I know which one," Pablo said at last, then opened the cabinet and brought out a small carving of a black bird. "Raven isn't one of the original fetishes our people carved, but an important lesson came to light as a result of its wisdom."

"Will you share the story with me, Uncle?" Gene asked, using the title to show respect, not because they were related.

Pablo looked around the store and, seeing they were alone, nodded. "It was at the time of the beginning," he said in a soft, compelling voice. "Raven and her friend were sitting on top of a mountain and, using their magic, began playing a game. They freed their eyes from their mortal bodies and sent them to specific points across the desert floor in a race of sorts. Mastery over all aspects of sight was part of Raven's magic, and one with their natures."

"So through their game, they honored who they were," Gene said with a nod.

"Exactly," Pablo said, "but Coyote was nearby, watching. After a while, he insisted that they teach *him* how to play. He refused to take no for an answer even though they repeatedly warned him of the danger. The Ravens eventually consented, but after plucking out his eyes, they flew away. Coyote waited in vain for his eyes to return, but that magic wasn't a part of him. Forced to do something at long last, Coyote replaced the eyes he'd lost with cranberries, which is why coyotes have yellow eyes and why their sight is poor.

"The lesson, of course," Pablo continued, "is that Raven's magic is not to be taken lightly. Raven brings the power of transformation to those willing to nurture their dreams. Raven lives in the inner world, a place of protection for that part of us that's most often injured by pain and rejection. Raven is a powerful ally who teaches us how to embrace the shadows, because they're also part of who we are."

"That's the perfect fetish for her," Gene said with a smile. "She'll take good care of it, too." Pablo wrapped it in a small box, but not before sprinkling a bit of corn pollen on it—a symbolic feeding.

After a short visit, Gene said goodbye and headed

back to his brother's sedan. He knew Lori would love it and, not wanting to wait to give it to her, decided a quick visit to the DMV was called for. Raven would help her as she faced today's challenges.

It would also give him an excuse to reassure himself that everything was okay. He still hadn't managed to get rid of that uneasiness, of the feeling that not all was as it should be.

Dismissing the thought, he headed over to the DMV.

Chapter Eighteen

As Gene approached the DMV's parking area, his blood turned to ice. One police car was in front of the entrance and a second in the alley, which was blocked off with yellow crime-scene tape. People were milling along the sidewalk and standing in clusters around the front of the building.

He recognized several people gathered around one of the police officers. They were all DMV employees.

Gene parked quickly, looking for Lori as he did, but he couldn't see her anywhere. Farther down he could see three more DMV employees gathered around another officer, but Lori wasn't with them, either.

Leaving his brother's sedan, Gene hurried over to the closest police officer.

"What's going on?" Gene asked, noting the familiar face.

"I wondered when you'd show up," Sergeant Chavez said, then called to a third officer who'd just arrived, asking him to keep watch over the alley and the back door of the office. Finally turning to Gene, he said, "I suppose you heard that Lori Baker's been kidnapped?"

Despite the sudden storm threatening to erupt inside his brain, he managed an exterior deadly calm. "I didn't know, not until this moment. Who did it—and how?"

"Sorry, I thought that's why you were here. Come inside with me. Take a look at the evidence and see if you have any theories."

Gene, trying to maintain his cool, followed the sergeant through a waist-high gate in the main counter that gave access to the employee area. Walking past several desks, they approached a small room at the back of the building. The wooden door to the lounge or staff break room, judging from the furnishings inside, had been badly damaged after being forcibly opened.

"This is as far as we can go. You can look from here, but nobody goes in except for the detectives and the crime-scene unit," Chavez said, holding up his hand to block Gene.

"How much do you know so far?" Gene asked, shifting to look past Chavez. There were signs of a struggle, with two metal chairs upended and the small table askew. At least one cup of coffee had been knocked onto the floor, and there was lipstick on the foam cup, Lori's shade of pink. At least there was no blood anywhere that he could see.

"From what the staff says, Ms. Baker came in

through the foyer wearing a wig today, but it obviously wasn't as good a disguise as she'd hoped," Chavez said.

"How did it go down? Did he come in through there?" Gene said, pointing to the steel door marked Employees Only Exit on the back wall of the break room. From what he could tell, it opened into the alley. There was a keypad for an electronic lock above the sturdy handle, but neither it nor the door itself showed any sign of damage or tampering.

"According to the staff, Ms. Baker took her break around ten-fifteen. She was in here alone, door closed, for about five minutes. Then one of the clerks heard what sounded like a yelp, a cut-off scream maybe. Two employees rushed over, but the door was jammed shut from the inside, with a chair against the knob. They forced it open, but that took almost a minute, and by then Ms. Baker was gone. Strangely enough, her purse is also missing."

"So she was taken out of here through the alley, which is why you have that area taped off." Gene sniffed the air, detecting an unusual odor. "What's that smell? It's chemical and familiar to me…."

"It's ether. It's used by truckers to help start cold engines. You can get it in most auto shops, and in a few high school chemistry labs, probably. We think Lori Baker was rendered unconscious, though she put up a struggle," Chavez said, gesturing around the room.

"Are there any surveillance cameras with a view of the front or the alley?"

Chavez shook his head. "Cameras are only in the service areas and the front parking lot. We'll be checking the feed for possible suspects—people who were outside or leaving the building around the time she disappeared."

"But right now you have nothing?" Gene pressed, his voice hard as he fought to keep his emotions buried.

"We don't have a suspect, if that's what you mean by nothing," he snapped, "but we have preliminary information. The rear door wasn't forced, so either she let a stranger in, which isn't likely, or she knew her kidnapper or kidnappers. It's also possible that someone knew the code and entered from the alley before or after she went on break. In that scenario, either the code was compromised or it was an inside job."

"Have you questioned all the employees and the customers here at the time?"

"We're in the process of doing that now, but so far, nobody saw anyone but Ms. Baker go into that room. A customer said that she saw someone in a white van racing out of the alley a little after ten, but she didn't notice the vehicle tags."

"Is there any chance that one of the outdoor cameras caught it?"

Chavez shook his head. "Wrong angle."

"What about coverage from a business across the

street, or maybe down the block?" Gene said, continuing to press.

"It's being handled." Chavez met Gene's gaze with a stony one of his own. "Let's get something straight right now. I *know* my job. I'm cutting you some slack and telling you what's what because your brother is with the department, but make no mistake. This is *our* case, and you need to back off and let us do our job."

Chavez escorted Gene outside, then walked away to talk to a detective who'd just arrived on the scene.

Gene watched for a moment. There was no way he was staying out of this. He still remembered what he'd told Lori when he'd dropped her off earlier that morning. The words clawed into him now.

He'd promised to watch her back and, one way or another, he intended to keep his promise.

LORI REGAINED CONSCIOUSNESS slowly and, as she did, realized that she was in a bedroom inside somebody's home, tied to a chair with what looked like drapery cord. Her thoughts were jumbled and, trying to lift the fog that clouded her senses, she shook her head.

She regretted that instantly. She had a world-class migraine, and there was one spot at the back of her head that throbbed with a vengeance.

She drew in a slow, steady breath to keep from vomiting, then looked around. The bed to her right held some embroidered throw pillows, evidence of a woman's touch. The room itself was sparsely furnished, with a cedar chest at the foot of the bed, and a small chest of drawers. It appeared to be a guest room.

Lori shifted, moving back and forth, trying to edge her chair closer to the door, but the legs of the chair thumped harder on the hardwood floor than she'd expected. She didn't make it far before she heard someone curse and the door was thrown open.

Lori stared at Steve Farmer, stunned. "*You,* Steve? *You're* the man who's been making my life crazy? But why? I've always tried to help you at work!"

He tossed her laptop and purse down onto the bed along with her cell phone. Lori could see the cell phone battery had been pulled, which meant nobody could track her location. But her laptop wasn't completely closed and she could see the display. It was powered up, which meant there was hope.

"You really have no idea?" Steve asked, a haunted look on his face.

"None," she said, tugging at the ropes that bound her wrists and held her to the chair. Steve had to be crazy. That was the only explanation that made sense. She had to find a way to get free or, worst-case scenario, buy time.

"Do you remember last Monday?" he said.

"What about it?"

"You took your break at the same time I did, and we sat at the table by the Coke machine. We each had our laptops out and I think you were blogging."

"This is about my blog? But I never write about work or mention any of my coworkers. It's only my random thoughts, and just on my webpage. What's it got to do with you?"

Steve held up a small flash drive. "Do you recognize this?"

"Yeah, it's a flash drive. So what's your point?"

He held it up close to her face. "It looks just like one of your flash drives, doesn't it? You use these to back up your current files before shutting down your computer."

"*So what?* A million other people do the same thing!" She stared at the device a moment longer. "Wait—are you saying that's *my* flash drive?"

"Now you're catching on."

Lori drew in a shaky breath. "Which would make the one I picked up, yours." She slowly began to realize the implications of that one mistake. "So that's why it wouldn't accept my files when I tried to back up later that night at home. It kept telling me the drive was full, which I knew wasn't true, so I just used a different flash drive. But what could possibly make your backup files so important that you'd risk getting killed over them, or killing someone else? Do you realize how many crimes you've committed for, what, a few megabytes of text?"

"Lori, shut up for a second," he snapped, then began pacing. "What you took from me was an *illegal* download. I stole Jerry's password and used his computer to get every licensed vehicle owner's address and social security number in this state."

She gasped. "Why would you do something like that? You can't possibly think you'd actually get away with it! You'll get fired for sure and probably serve jail time."

"That's *my* problem. I'm doing what I have to do. You wouldn't be part of this at all if you hadn't walked off with my flash drive. I really tried to keep you out of this, too. I did everything I could, from snatching your purse to searching your house and car."

"Why didn't you just ask me for it?"

"And risk having you connect me to an illegal download? You'd check to make sure, then I'd be screwed. You'd turn me in."

"I never tried to access the files, so I had no idea it was your flash drive," she said. "I just assumed the memory chip had gone south somehow—been corrupted."

"I was so sure you'd figure it out, but when you didn't say or do anything, I assumed my luck was still holding. I planned to sneak up and grab your purse after you left the restaurant that first night. I knew that you'd had a problem with Harrington, and he and I are the same size, so I dressed like he did and hoped the disguise would throw you off."

"It worked. I was sure it was him...."

"Then you got mixed up with that Navajo man. I tracked down his name later and looked up everyone associated with him. It was easy to check on next of kin, since out here almost everyone owns a car or truck," he said. "I never intended on hurting you, Lori. All I ever wanted was to get that flash drive back—without letting you know it was me. That's why I also switched Harrington's plates around, to confuse you."

"But you put my life in danger, Steve. Duane Hays came after me with a gun—and he didn't miss by much."

"I know. When I heard about it on the news, I couldn't believe what he'd done. I told him not to hurt you. Then I got worried that he'd somehow end up identifying me to the cops. There was no way I could risk getting arrested, not before I got those files back. So I went to work early this morning to try and download the information again. I was ready to search Jerry's office from top to bottom until I found his new password. I also brought a hand towel and a can of ether I got from an auto shop just in case I ran into Harvey. Fortunately, he was having breakfast in his car and never even saw me. Nobody else came in early, so I had plenty of time, but I still couldn't find Jerry's new password."

"You conned me about that client with the ex-wife back at the DMV, didn't you?" she realized, putting the final pieces together in her head. "You were hoping to get any password that would let you download those files again."

"Yes, but it didn't work, so I had to think of something else."

"Like coming after me?"

"It was my last chance," Steve said. "I called in sick and waited in a van outside until just before your usual break time. I sneaked in through the back exit and was hiding behind the cola machine when you came in. The rest, well, you went out like a light once I was able to get that ether-soaked towel over your mouth and nose."

"You've done all this for what—money, revenge, politics?"

"No, this was never about money or any of that other crap." He ran a hand through his hair and paced back and forth, continuing to take quick, furtive glances out the window. "The reason I couldn't come to you has nothing to do with me getting caught. They kidnapped my wife, and unless I deliver what they want, they'll kill Sue. I have until midnight tonight to give them those files."

She swallowed hard. *Now* things were finally starting to make some sense. "*Who* has her? Do you have any idea?" she pressed.

"No, that's why I'm stuck playing this game. I told them that I had the data, then after you got my flash drive I had to call them back and explain what had happened. They gave me more time, but warned me not to tell you what was going on. Now if I can't produce another flash drive with the stuff by tonight, Sue's dead." His voice cracked and he rubbed a hand over his face, wiping away errant tears.

"*Why* haven't you called the police?"

"That's the first thing they told me not to do— and they're watching me, Lori. They know when I get to the office, what I do there, when I leave work, what I do afterward. If I got anyone else involved, they threatened to do things to Sue...." He swallowed hard. "That's why I nearly panicked when an officer showed up at my door fifteen minutes ago asking about you."

"What did you say to him?"

"I told him I hadn't seen you, and got rid of him fast."

"The police will return. Then what will you do?"

"I'll do anything to get my wife back, but I'm not out to hurt you, Lori," he said. "Just to show you that I'm telling the truth, I'm going to cut you loose. But don't run. Sue's life is on the line and they're outside somewhere, watching. Do you understand?" He brought out a pocketknife and started to work on the cords behind her back.

She nodded. "Steve, we've *got* to get help. You're clearly no match for the people you're up against."

"Give me the flash drive and I'll take care of the rest."

Lori swallowed hard. Steve was on the brittle edge, and when she told him what she'd done with that drive, things were bound to get a lot worse.

Playing for time, she stood and took off the wig

she'd been wearing. It was tugging at her scalp and making it hard for her to think. "Let me call my friend," Lori pleaded in a soft voice. "He can help us. His brother is a security expert and his other brother has his own detective agency. They're *not* the police."

He shook his head. "If anyone shows up here unexpectedly, I have no idea what they'll do to Sue. I won't take a chance with her life. Having you here is risky enough."

Lori swallowed hard. "Are they outside right now?" Seeing him nod, she added, "Show me."

"No. Stay away from the windows. Let's go into the hall to talk. Nobody can see us from the outside."

DANIEL HEARD A KNOCK AT HIS front door. "That's Paul. I'll let him in," he told Gene.

A moment later Paul and Dan walked over and joined Gene, who was busy working at one of the computers.

"What's going on?" Paul asked.

"I've got a lead," Gene said, never taking his eyes off the screen. "I think I know who Lori's kidnapper is. Whoever came in through the back door had to have known the access code on the lock. I spoke to Miranda, Lori's friend at the DMV, and she gave me the names of the two employees who were absent today. One's the department supervisor, Jerry Esteban, who's supposedly on vacation, and then there's

Steve Farmer, who called in sick. Farmer is about the same size as Harrington and has the right shape. I think he's our man, but the only problem is that Farmer has no motive that I can see."

"Let the police handle this. They're trained—you're not. If they haven't been to interview Farmer yet, they will," Paul said.

Gene shook his head. "Unless they see some sign of Lori at Farmer's place they can't do a thing. To get a search warrant they'll need probable cause. They'll just move on to the next thing on their list, finding and questioning Jerry Esteban, and that'll take hours, considering he's abroad on vacation," Gene said, then continued in a hard voice. "I'm not playing by the rules on this. I'm going to Farmer's home right now to check things out for myself."

"Not alone, you're not," Daniel said in a stony voice.

"You've got that right," Paul said.

Gene glanced at his brothers. "Okay, you can help, but once we find whoever has Lori, he's mine."

Gene leaned back and showed them the information he had on-screen. "Here's what I've got so far on Steve Farmer—address, wife's name, relatives, background, etc."

"Did either of you try to track Lori's cell phone GPS and maybe confirm her location?" Paul asked.

"Yeah, I did that, while Gene was working on this computer, but I had no luck," Dan said. "My guess is that Farmer pulled the battery from her phone."

Gene looked up at Dan quickly. "Lori's got anti-theft tracking software installed in her laptop, remember? She showed us the CD software case after the break-in at her house," he said. "Is it possible for you to track that? She carries the laptop to work in her tote bag, and that disappeared along with her."

"I remember the brand." Dan considered it for a moment, then nodded. "I've done work with the security people connected to that software company. Since I've already got Lori's full name and address, it may be possible for me to get the location of her laptop," Dan said. "Step back and give me some room. I need to work around some normal procedures."

It took several minutes and a software download, but eventually the screen shifted, becoming an elaborate map, then its focus narrowed twice. "Lori Baker's laptop computer is at 424 Oak Street," Dan said.

"That's Farmer's home address," Gene said. "Let's go."

"No, we can't go bursting in there without a plan," Paul said.

"Getting Lori back safely is what really counts now," Dan said. "I know you like going through channels, Paul, but if we call the police, and they actually buy into this, it'll still take them an hour to assemble a team and make their move."

"We can't afford delays," Gene said. "Farmer is unpredictable."

"What has Lori told you about that guy?" Paul asked Gene.

"Nothing, but I'm certain that if he'd caused her any problems, she would have said so."

Daniel switched screens, typed in a password and entered an encrypted site. "Farmer's got no criminal record whatsoever—not even a parking ticket. He's married and squeaky clean."

"Then what's he doing with Lori's laptop computer? Let's go pay him a visit," Gene said.

"Wait," Paul said, pushing Gene back down into the chair. "Pull up the house on Google, Dan, and let's see the layout there."

Chapter Nineteen

Twenty minutes later, they approached Farmer's home. Gene nodded to Daniel, who, like him, was wearing a tan uniform work shirt and a phony photo ID tag around his neck.

Paul, at the wheel of the van and wearing a white shirt and tie, spoke as they passed Steve's residence. "That's the place. If he's home, his van must be in the garage."

"The curtains are closed, but I saw a light on inside," Gene said. "A bedroom or maybe the kitchen."

Daniel handed Gene a white hard hat that matched the one he was putting on. "The gas company headgear is blue, but these will have to do."

The hard hat felt a little big to Gene, but there was no time to do any adjusting and he wouldn't need it for long. The handheld radio was far more critical, and he checked the unit on his belt again.

Paul slowed, made the turn at the end of the block, then stopped at the alley that separated the backyards of the eight houses on the block.

He steadied the big basket of flowers on the seat beside him. "Okay, this is it, guys. I'll circle back around and pull into the Farmer driveway close to the garage, blocking the way. Once you're in position, give me the go-ahead call and I'll deliver these flowers. Listen in and when you hear me say 'Johnson,' make your entry one way or the other."

"Copy that," Daniel said as he opened the side door of the van and jumped out. Gene followed, carrying two shovels, part of their cover. Paul drove off immediately as they began their walk down the alley.

As they reached the back gate, Gene felt his stomach tighten. Knowing Lori was in danger was eating him up inside. He'd wasted so much time. Despite the iron grip he'd always had on his emotions, he'd fallen head over heels in love with Lori, and there was no turning back.

He'd fight for her, maybe even bleed for her, but to hold on to Lori he'd need to show her how he felt. Then the next move would be up to her. He'd accept her gratitude for the help he'd given her, but he wouldn't use that to bind her. He wanted her heart—nothing less.

Gene unfastened the catch and opened the gate, and Dan followed him in. While Dan brought the yellow Taser out of its holster and thumbed the button on his radio, Gene continued to inch along the wall, careful to stay out of sight. When they reached the back door, they stopped and waited, listening for Paul's signal.

Gene heard a doorbell, then silence followed for about thirty seconds. After that, heavy footsteps came from somewhere inside the house.

"Hello, I have a delivery for Mrs. Johnson."

Hearing the signal, Gene kicked the back door just below the knob as hard as he could. The force hurled it open and Gene rushed in, Daniel right behind him.

As Gene stormed into the living room, Steve Farmer, trying to evade Paul, ran straight toward him. Gene tackled him to the floor, then brought his fist back.

"No!" Lori yelled, stepping into view from the hall. "It's not his fault. You need to hear him out."

Cursing, Gene hauled Farmer up.

"He's *not* the bad guy in all this," Lori said quickly. "His wife's been kidnapped, and he's been trying to save her. We've got to help Steve or she'll die."

As THEY TOOK SEATS AROUND the living room, Gene finally saw the cut-up rope sections on the sofa that Steve had used to tie Lori up.

He jumped to his feet. "You tied her up?" he bellowed, moving for Steve.

Lori grabbed Gene's arm and held him back. "It's not important now. Someone's life is at stake."

"No, it *is* too late," Steve said, tears forming

in his eyes and his voice cracking. "I'm sure they either saw or heard you guys bursting in here. Sue's as good as dead."

"No, don't assume that," Lori said quickly. "The guys broke in through the *back,* so maybe the kidnappers didn't see them. Don't give up hope," Lori said and quickly explained what Steve had done and why.

"How sure are you that they're watching you?" Paul asked, going to the window and peering out through a small gap in the curtains. "I didn't see anyone when I drove around the block or pulled up, and nobody was sitting in any of the cars parked in or around the driveways on this street."

"They always seem to know where I'm at. They have to have someone keeping an eye on me. I often see a green pickup—a Ford 150—so maybe that's them."

"I'll drive off in the van, then park in the alley and have a look around," Paul said. "If anyone's watching the house, I'll spot them."

"Be careful," Daniel said.

As Paul walked out, Lori looked at Gene, and the tender emotions mirrored in his steady gaze took her breath away. Today, she'd seen the bear unleashed, but this other side of Gene just drew her to him even more.

"They're out there," Steve repeated dully.

"We'll know soon enough," Gene growled at him.

While Daniel watched Steve, Gene took Lori's hand and led her into the hall.

As soon as they were out of view, Gene pulled her into his arms. Covering her mouth with his, he forced her lips open and drank her in with the desperation of a man long denied.

When he eased his hold at long last, her legs nearly buckled. Her entire body was throbbing with need and awareness. "Wow," she managed in a shaky voice. "Whatever happened to the slow-moving man I've come to know? First, you charge into the room, and now...that kiss...well, wow!"

"A man has only so much restraint.... After that, all bets are off."

She bit her bottom lip and smiled slowly. "I like this side of you very much," she whispered.

He brought her against him once again, kissing her with a force that rocked everything she'd thought she'd known about him.

"I can't get enough of you," he said, his breath hot on her lips.

She steadied herself by leaning against him, but before she could say or do anything, Paul came into the hall, having returned through the back.

"Okay, you two, save it for later. We've got a problem."

Feeling guilty, Lori immediately moved away from Gene and focused. Steve Farmer and his wife needed their help now. This was no time for distractions of any kind.

As she and Gene joined the others in the living room, Lori saw Steve sunken down in the sofa, his eyes hollow and empty. He looked completely defeated.

"What's happened?" she asked quickly.

"When I walked to the van I saw a green Ford pickup with two men inside parked across the street, half a block down. It wasn't there when we arrived, so it hasn't been there for long. I backed out into the street, and a second later, they casually drove off in the opposite direction," Paul said. "I waited until they were out of sight, then parked in the alley. They won't be able to see me from the street now."

"Doesn't matter. They'll kill her—if they haven't already," Steve whispered.

"You're not seeing things in the right light," Paul said. "What they saw was a flower delivery man, and they drove off before I could get a look. They didn't want anyone in the neighborhood to be able to give the cops a description of them."

"What if they took off because they thought *you* were a cop?" Steve asked.

Paul shook his head. "A cop wouldn't have left your house so soon and alone, then allow them to drive off without going after them."

Steve nodded at last. "If you're right, then maybe Sue still has a chance," he said, then looked at Lori. "You've got to give me that flash drive."

She took a deep breath, wishing with all her heart

that she could have avoided telling him the truth. "Steve, I'm really sorry, but when I couldn't get the flash drive to load up my files, I assumed it was corrupted. I threw it out, and trash pickup was the day before yesterday."

"What?" He jumped to his feet and stepped toward her. Gene instantly blocked his way.

"Sit down," he snapped, grabbing Steve's arm firmly.

Steve took a step back, then seemed to crumple into the chair. "I can't do this anymore. I'm going out there to find them. If they're going to kill Sue, they might as well put a bullet in me, too."

"Don't think like that," Lori said. "You're not in this alone anymore. What we have to do now is find a way to turn the tables on them." She was scared, but she also felt a terrible sense of responsibility for what was happening to Steve and what might happen to Sue. Logically, she knew it hadn't been her fault. She'd had no idea what was going on.

Yet when she looked at Steve now, all she could feel was sympathy. She couldn't just sit back and hope everything would somehow turn out okay.

"Let's start with what we know," Lori said. "They've got you under surveillance, but it's not around-the-clock, so it's possible that they still don't realize what's really going on. Let's find out for sure."

"What do you have in mind?" Despite Steve's weary voice, he was now sitting up a little straighter.

"We need the kidnappers to come out of hiding and I think I know a way to do that," she said. "Steve and I will leave in the van," Lori said, then looked at Steve. "It's in the garage, right?"

He nodded. "It was the only way I could get you into the house without my neighbors seeing."

"When you pull out this time, Steve, I'll be sitting beside you, like I'm being coerced and have been convinced to cooperate. If they're back again and watching, they'll pick up on us," Lori said.

"You and Steve alone? No way," Gene said.

"Then come with us. Ride in the back and be sure to keep your head down," she said.

Paul shook his head. "Slow down, guys. No one's going anywhere yet. Give me a chance to get a few things together." He met Steve's gaze. "You'll be wearing an ankle bracelet, so if you bolt and decide to go on solo, we'll find you," he said, his eyes drilling holes into him.

"After Paul returns with the gear, he and I will follow Steve's van but stay well back," Daniel said. "If you pick up a tail, we'll let you know. From that point on, the objective will be to find out where they're hiding Sue."

Lori saw the trapped look on Steve's face. "This will buy us some time," she said. "If the kidnappers call, tell them that I'm taking you to where I left the flash drive. It'll work, you'll see."

Daniel looked at Paul. "The next move's yours,

bro. Go get what we need. Make sure you come back with more flowers, too, as if you made a mistake on your first trip, just in case they're back, watching."

"Do you really think this will work?" Steve asked Lori, his tone hopeful for the first time.

"We'll get her back, Steve," she said. "We're all on your side."

Paul was gone for forty minutes and time seemed to drag, turning each second into a small eternity. With every passing moment, Steve's panic grew.

Lori wanted to reach out to him, to help him somehow, but there was nothing she could say to him now. The thought of losing his wife was slowly killing him. As she watched Steve, she wondered if love was actually worth the aching sense of vulnerability that always seemed to go with it.

WHEN PAUL RETURNED, HE came in through the front with another big bouquet and a shopping bag this time. Moments later, Paul removed the ankle bracelet from the bag and slipped it around Steve's leg.

"If you run, I'll find you," Paul said, his eyes and voice expressionless as he activated the device. "This is necessary because you're scared and not thinking straight. Your best hope of getting your wife back safely is to work with, not against, us. Remember that."

"Let's load up," Gene said, once Paul was done.

"Follow the van, guys, but be careful. Don't get spotted."

"We won't," Daniel said. "No one will see us, but we'll be there."

Gene, Lori and Steve went out through the kitchen into the garage and climbed into the van.

"I'll stay back here," Gene said, crouching down as Steve pushed the remote and opened the garage bay door.

"You had a maroon van at the beginning of all this, didn't you?" Lori asked Steve.

"Yeah, but I traded it off in a really bad deal at one of those used-car lots out on East Main. I needed to keep you off balance."

"I wish you'd have come to me right away," Lori said, "but never mind. We're on your side now and we'll move heaven and earth to help you get Sue back safe and sound."

"This is my fault. If I'd only applied for a job else-where…"

"No. Stop. This is *not* your fault. Sue's kidnappers are the guilty ones." Yet even as she spoke, she could tell that he didn't believe her. "You can't take the blame for decisions you didn't make," she said, thinking of what had happened between her parents as well as Steve's present situation.

"I just want her back," Steve said, his voice unsteady. "Have you ever been so much in love that you'd rather die than see the other person hurt?"

"Love can be the most wonderful feeling in the

world," she said, deliberately not answering his question, "but it always comes at a price."

He nodded, but said nothing else.

Lori felt Gene's gaze on her, but he never said a word.

Chapter Twenty

They'd been driving around for about thirty minutes when Daniel, now alone in the other van, called
Gene. "You've got a tail. Green Ford pickup. It's
hanging back but keeping pace with you. Paul's
driving on a parallel street, and he confirmed that
it's the same one he saw earlier."

"Let's make sure the truck's tailing us, not just
driving on the same street," Gene said, then told
Steve to take a hard right.

A second later, Daniel spoke. "He's still there,
but neither Paul nor I can close in. There's too much
traffic at the intersection I'm at, and Paul's a block
over."

"I've got an idea," Gene said. Putting Daniel on
speaker, Gene told Steve to head down the next alley
between the small Spanish bakery and the tire shop.
"Once we're in there, slow down just enough for
me to jump out. I'll hide behind the trash bin while
you go a little farther and park sideways, blocking
the way. Then I want you to haul Lori out of the car
and act as if you plan to rough her up." He paused,

then in a low voice added, "Make it look good, but if you hurt her in any way, I'll make you wish you were never born. You get me?"

"Yeah, yeah, okay," Steve said.

As they drove down the alley Gene saw a line of big industrial trash bins on his left. "Once I'm out, don't look in my direction and ignore the green Ford. Somebody else will be watching it. If all goes well, we'll soon know where these guys are keeping your wife."

Steve slowed enough to allow Gene to jump out. As he did, several pigeons scattered but remained on the ground as Gene ran behind the bins.

Crouching low and out of sight, Gene watched the van continue on for about fifty yards, then come to a full stop. Steve yanked Lori out the driver's side and pulled her into the shadows.

Lori yelled something and ran into the alley, but Steve pulled her back while she appeared to struggle.

Although they were doing a great acting job, Gene couldn't see the green pickup anywhere. Trying to mask out their phony argument, Gene listened for the sound of an approaching vehicle.

Finally losing patience, he slipped out from cover and made his way to the end of the alley for a quick look around. The Ford pickup was parked across the street and the driver appeared to be watching the action through binoculars, his own face hidden.

As the pickup's driver swung the binoculars in

Gene's direction, Gene ducked back instantly, then moved back down the alley, out of view. All he could do now was hope he hadn't been spotted.

Several heart-stopping minutes passed before Gene heard a vehicle roaring up the alley. The pigeons all took flight, wings fluttering in panic mode.

Gene looked around the corner of the Dumpster and realized that the pickup was racing straight toward him. He'd be crushed between the trash bin and the wall.

"No!" Lori's scream pierced the air.

As he turned his head, he saw her run straight at the pickup and, at the last second, hurl a rock directly at its windshield.

The rock bounced off the glass and the pickup swerved, catching the big trash bin with its fender instead of head-on. The force of impact slammed the heavy metal container into Gene, hurling him back. He bounced off the brick wall and fell onto the pavement.

For a second, Gene's vision grayed, but anger gave him the energy he needed and he managed to get back on his feet. Lori was nowhere to be seen, but the pickup was just ahead. The driver placed the truck into Reverse, did a one-eighty and raced out of the alley.

His body ached, but the only thing on his mind was Lori. As he took some shaky steps forward, he saw her sprawled on the ground, facedown, completely still. His body turned cold, and as he ran to her side he felt nothing except a bone-deep terror.

He was only a few feet away when he saw her move. Relief exploded through him. He couldn't breathe, he couldn't speak. He crouched down and checked her over gently. To his surprise, there wasn't a mark on her. She rolled over onto her back and looked up at him, terror in her eyes.

"I hugged the ground and stayed as flat as I could," she said, trying not to cry but failing.

"Are you hurt?" he asked, his voice unsteady.

"No, I'm okay," she said, sitting up.

With a groan, he drew her against him and held her tightly.

"You're crushing me," she gasped.

He eased his hold instantly. "You make me crazy," he growled. "You should have stayed back. I would have figured something out." Yet, even as he spoke, he knew that he would have probably been dead by now if she hadn't distracted the driver.

"You were pinned in with no place to go! What did you expect me to do?" she asked, nuzzling into him.

He sucked in a jagged breath as pain shot through him.

She pulled away. "*You're* hurt!"

"And Sue is as good as dead now," Steve said as he approached. "Now they know you guys are involved, and there's nothing else I can do."

Before Gene could answer, Daniel pulled into the

alley and came to a stop with a screech of brakes. "Paul's circling, trying to locate the pickup," he shouted, climbing out of the van. "You okay, bro?"

"I'm fine," Gene said quickly. "My shoulder took a hit, but it's not dislocated."

"I couldn't get over in time to block the pickup before it got away. Unless Paul gets lucky, we're going to need a new plan," Daniel said, his eyes still on Gene. "Are you sure you don't need to go to the E.R.?"

"I'm fine."

"Maybe *you* are, but we blew it, and now Sue's going to pay," Steve said in a curiously flat voice.

Gene glanced at the man and could have sworn that Steve had aged ten years in the last ten minutes. "You're forgetting one thing, Steve, and you need to hang on to this. Sue's valuable to them because she's a means to an end. What they want is the information they forced you to get. These guys are probably the ones responsible for the rash of identity thefts in our area. So hang tough, because I'm sure we haven't heard the last of them."

"He's right," Dan said. "From the response they saw here today, they also know that the cops aren't involved yet. You've kept that part of the deal, so in their minds they still have a chance to get what they're after."

"Maybe so," Steve said, his weary voice betraying the tug-of-war between hope and fear that was going on inside him. "So what do we do now?"

"We wait for them to contact you again," Daniel said. "I'll ride with you back to your house." Daniel looked at Lori. "Take my truck and drive my brother to an E.R. so he can have his shoulder looked at. Just don't say what really happened, or the doctor will want to call the cops." He tossed Lori his keys. "The kidnappers will keep their eye on Steve because he's their main asset. I'll link up with Paul and have him tail us back to Steve's house."

As soon as Steve and Daniel got under way, Lori hurried with Gene back to the pickup.

"I'll get you to the E.R. as quickly as I can," she said.

"Not necessary," he said. "I've had broken bones and dislocated my shoulder before. The pain isn't at the same level now. Sure, I took a hit, but the worst of it is that I'll have a rough time lifting bales for the next few weeks. Forget about it and let's get going."

"Where? To Steve's?"

"No, that's exactly where we shouldn't go. We want the kidnappers to ease up, and a crowd at Steve's place is going to do the exact opposite." He paused, thinking it over. "Head over to Preston's."

She placed Daniel's truck in gear. As she drove, she kept shooting Gene quick, worried glances.

"Trust me, I'm fine," he said.

"I still say that Daniel's right. You should have that looked at."

"I'll tell you what. You can look me over once we're at Preston's."

She smiled, the words teasing her imagination and making her skin prickle. "Okay, you're on, but if anything looks really off, you're going to the E.R. Agreed?"

"Deal."

As Lori wove her way through traffic, Gene thought back to what had happened in the alley. Lori had stepped right out into the path of an oncoming truck, ready to die in order to save his life. That one act had left him far more shaken than the bruise on his shoulder. "What you did today..."

"You'd have done for me—though your arm would probably be better if my aim didn't suck," she added with a sheepish smile. "I wanted to shatter the windshield right in front of the driver, but I missed and hit the passenger side."

"Close enough," he said. Lori was a handful of trouble, and she never did what he expected her to do. She questioned everything and had some serious baggage, but she understood him better than anyone else ever had. She also loved and valued the things he did, including his ranch, and was willing to risk everything to do what she thought was right. Lori could comfort him with her silence—though admittedly those moments were few—and make him laugh. His life would never be the same without her. Tonight he would show her just how much she meant to him.

"What's that smile about?" she asked.

"I have plans," he said, then steadfastly refused to answer any more questions.

When they arrived at Preston's a short time later, Gene used his key and hurried her inside. "No one followed us. I kept looking in the rearview mirror," she said.

"I know. I did the same thing. For now, we're safe," he said, flipping on the lights. "I'm going to call Dan and Paul and let them know where we are."

"What happens now?"

"We wait until Steve's contacted. The way I figure it, they'll turn up the pressure on him a notch or two, making more threats directed at his wife, but they'll be in touch soon."

She dropped her purse down onto a chair. "Okay, let me take a look at your shoulder—and, remember, you agreed that if I didn't like the looks of it, you'd go with me to the E.R."

He gave her a slow smile. "So come take my shirt off and have a look."

He heard her sigh as she drew closer to him. Then, standing in front of him, she began to work the buttons of his shirt, her hands trembling slightly.

"Let me know if you see something you like," he said, tucking a strand of honey-brown hair behind her ear. He smiled as he saw her try to suppress a shiver.

"It doesn't look bad, though you've got the beginnings of a very colorful bruise," she said. As she slid his shirt away from his shoulders, her hands brushed his skin in a light caress.

He hissed in a breath.

"Did I hurt you?" she asked quickly.

"Darling, hurt's the last thing I'm feeling right now, but just so there's no mistake..." He held her face in his hands, then took her mouth roughly, parting her lips, and loving the soft inside with his tongue.

As Lori rubbed her body against his, he groaned, and his kiss turned even hotter. He plundered her mouth, drinking in the taste of her until it became one with his own.

At last he drew in a breath. "Fair's fair," he murmured. "I have no shirt on. Take off yours."

"You want it off, then you do it," she said, stepping back, her eyes burning.

That soft challenge was his undoing. With need pounding through him, he pulled her closer, then tugged at her shirt and bra, tossing them aside. He kissed her breasts, loving the way she sighed.

He was too hot. He had to draw back and slow down, but when he eased his hold, she whimpered softly.

"More."

That one word tore through him like a bolt of lightning. She was ready for him and that's all he needed to know. Dropping to his knees, he pulled her slacks and panties down, then left a moist trail down the center of her body with the tip of his tongue. He loved the way he could make her gasp and quiver, but before he could finish what he'd begun, she took an unsteady step back.

"My legs won't hold me if you keep doing that," she managed.

Laughing softly, he wrapped his arms tightly around her and guided her down onto the bed. "I won't let you fall, little raven. Before tonight's over, you'll fly."

Standing by the side of the bed, he unbuckled his belt and discarded his jeans. As he took a step toward her, she shook her head.

"No, wait. Let me look at you first," she said, her gaze devouring him, fueling the heat inside him.

He remained where he was, fighting the fire coursing through his veins, until she opened her arms to him.

"We'll start slow and easy, but I'm too hot, so things won't stay that way for long," he whispered, lying beside her.

He kissed her deeply, wanting to burn tonight into her memory. He loved Lori and he needed to show her what was in his heart. Words weren't enough.

"I've never felt like this," she said, gasping for breath as he parted her folds and caressed her there. "Everything is so…intense."

"Just let go," he whispered in her ear.

"I…need you so much!" she said, her body arching and peaking with pleasure.

"You've got me." He waited until her breathing

evened once again. The way she came alive for him made him crazy.

Unable to wait any longer, he entered her slowly and, trying not to hurt her, moved gently, in rhythm with her own body. He wanted everything she could give him, now, while he could still think.

Gene slipped one hand between them and touched her in a way he knew would drive her wild. With a cry, she came apart for him.

He felt her tighten around him and fire spilled into his blood. He drove deep and hard into her, heat blinding him as he followed her over that brittle edge.

As his breathing evened, he gazed down at her and saw Lori smile. It was the lazy, thoroughly contented look of a woman who'd been well loved.

Gene shifted so he could lie beside her, and as he did, he saw her gaze drift over him.

"How's your shoulder?" she asked, worrying her bottom lip.

"What shoulder?"

She smiled. "You're so beautiful naked."

He laughed. "Nobody's ever called me beautiful—naked or otherwise."

"You are," she said, lying on her side, stroking his stomach muscles and the coarse hairs on the lower part of his belly. "What we shared...it was amazing. No one's ever made me feel that way before."

"Everything was right between us, *sawe*," he said, pulling her against him.

"*Sawe?*"

"It means sweetheart," he answered.

"Before, you called me raven," she said, remembering. "Why raven? My hair's not black."

"Raven's your spiritual sister," he said, then stood and reached for his slacks.

Digging into one of his pockets, he returned to the bed and held out a small box. "This is now yours, something to add to your medicine pouch." He waited until she opened it, then continued. "Raven is your ally, and a source of power to you." He told her the story of Raven, then continued. "The spirit of Raven will teach you how to soar above all the shadows that follow you."

"This is such a beautiful gift. Thank you," she said, leaning over to kiss him.

After placing the small fetish into her leather pouch, Lori lay beside Gene once again. "Tonight I loved and was loved in return," she said softly. "And now I have something that will always remind me of tonight."

"And should you ever lose your way, trust Raven to show you the way back into my arms."

Chapter Twenty-One

They fell asleep, her head resting on his chest, but sometime later Gene's cell phone rang, jolting them awake. He picked it up on the second ring.

"The kidnappers called," Daniel said quickly. "We're trying to trace the call, but Paul's not optimistic. He's sure it'll be a burn phone, and the most his source will be able to get is the closest cell tower."

"What's their new demand?" Gene asked.

"They still want the files, but they'll only trade if Steve can deliver the information before morning. They ordered us to meet them at a private landfill west of town."

"So what now?" Gene asked.

"Come back to Steve's. We need to talk."

"There's more to this, isn't there, something you're not telling me?" Gene said, reading his brother's guarded tone.

"Just make sure you're not followed. Go through the easement along the side of the house and park there."

"All right," Gene said, then placed the phone down.

"What time is it?" Lori asked sleepily.

"A little past midnight." Gene looked at her. She was so beautiful he wished he could have made love to her again. He kissed her one last time, took a breath and got out of bed.

"The kidnappers called. It's time for us to go."

THEY ARRIVED AT STEVE'S PLACE thirty minutes later, coming up the alley, and Daniel let them into the house. From what Gene could see, they'd done some repairs to make the back door functional, though it was far from secure.

"Update me," Gene said.

"The kidnappers are using a throwaway phone, as Paul's contact thought, so we can't get a location. Steve's supposed to meet with them just before daybreak, so we've got a few hours to come up with a plan."

Once in the kitchen, Lori caught the scent of coffee. Following her nose, she poured two cups of the dark brew and offered Gene one.

"We have to break into the DMV and download the information they want," Steve said, his voice loud and strained. "Without that we'll never get Sue back alive."

"That place is too secure to hit without more time and resources. We'll end up in jail with no chance of rescuing your wife," Paul said. "We have to find another way."

Steve ran a hand through his hair. "I can't think straight anymore. Maybe another cup of coffee will help," he said, picking up his empty mug. "Anyone else?"

They shook their heads.

"What's our next move?" Gene said as soon as Steve left the room.

Paul and Daniel exchanged quick glances, and that confirmed Gene's suspicions. Something *was* up. Gene looked at Daniel, who looked away. Just then, they heard the back door close.

With a curse, Paul bolted out of his chair, shot through the kitchen and headed outside.

Gene followed him, but he didn't have to go far. Paul tackled Steve before he reached the gate.

Steve didn't resist as he was hauled to his feet and taken back inside.

"I could track you anywhere with that ankle bracelet," Paul said. "Where did you think you were going?"

"I was going to call my wife's kidnappers, tell them I had the data they wanted and arrange a meet. So what if it was a lie? If they kill me and Sue, at least we'd go together."

Lori felt her heart go out to him. Love could make you do things you never thought yourself capable of doing. She remembered what Steve had said about being willing to die rather than seeing the woman he loved hurt.

She felt the same way about Gene; that's why she'd risked her life to protect him in that alley. She hadn't meant to fall in love, not this completely. She'd meant to hold back, but love didn't need permission to exist. It simply happened when you least expected it.

As she looked at Steve she felt waves of compassion washing over her.

"We're on your side, Steve," Daniel said. "The key to keeping Sue and Lori safe is to get the kidnappers the data they want. Now we have to figure out a way to do that."

"Wait—*Lori?*" Gene said and glared at his brothers. "What's she got to do with this?"

"The kidnappers are willing to trade the flash drive for Sue, but only if Lori delivers it," Daniel said.

"Why me?" Lori asked, confused.

"I think they're worried that you got a look at the driver who tried to crush me in that alley," Gene said. "You've become a liability to them. That's why you can't go."

"But I didn't see the man. I was too busy hugging the ground," Lori said. "Maybe they just see me as less dangerous than Steve."

"What if you're wrong? We can't risk trading one hostage for another," Gene said, glaring at his brothers.

"I have a plan that should keep both women safe," Daniel said.

"Lori can't be part of it," Gene said.

She placed a hand on Gene's arm. "What's your plan, Daniel?" she asked.

"There's one place I can access that has computers powerful enough to hack into the DMV's database. I'm in charge of checking out current firewalls and internet security at the tribe's natural gas plant, and that's something that has to be done when the day shift is off duty to avoid complications. I'll take Lori with me because she's familiar with the system the DMV uses."

"Then I'm going, too," Gene said.

"Okay. I'll tell the guard that you two are going to help me perform a multiuser simulated attack to verify security measures protecting the network."

"That's a mouthful," Gene said.

"It's part of what I do," Daniel said. "Once we're there I have some high-end password-breaking programs I can try. There won't be anyone looking over our shoulders. If Lori can give me an idea of what Jerry's used in the past, we can try to find the new password by taking some major shortcuts."

"Jerry's last password was the name of his dog," Steve said.

"Then I'll need the name of all his pets, past and present. Do you know them?" he asked Steve.

"I do," Lori said. "Not all, but most. He uses names from Greek mythology, like Zeus and so on."

"That'll help. Are you ready?" Seeing them nod, Daniel headed to the door. "Let's go. Paul can stay here with Steve."

THEY ARRIVED AT THE PLANT just as the last of the midnight shift was passing through security. Having discussed their strategy during the trip onto the Navajo Nation site, they each knew what to do.

The guard at the first of two gas refinery security gates recognized Daniel as he pulled up and stopped.

"Evening, Dan. Still working on those off-hours security checks?" the guard asked, smiling. Leaning over to check out the other passengers, he added, "Hey, that you, Gene?"

Gene recognized Miles Nakai from his high school days on the Rez. "Yeah, Miles. Dan didn't say you worked here. How you doing?" he said, bringing out his driver's license as identification. "We're helping my brother with his antihacker tests tonight. He's been bellyaching about having to handle three keyboards at the same time, so we're the hired help. This is Lori Baker. She has a lot of hands-on experience and is a friend of mine."

Myles inspected Lori's driver's license and DMV badge, then Daniel's ID, according to procedure. "Okay, go on through," he said, opening the electronic gate and waving them in.

Three minutes later, they were alone, walking down an interior corridor.

"Hey, bro, you're a natural," Daniel whispered.

"If this ever comes back at you, blame it all on me," Gene said. "Tell them that I forced you at gunpoint—whatever. I'll take the heat."

"Will you shut up?" Daniel growled. "I'm in this to the end with both of you."

Lori blinked back tears. "This is my fault. I got you two involved. I don't know how I'll ever be able to repay you."

Gene wrapped his arm around her shoulders, drawing her closer. "A simple thanks to my brother will be enough," he said, then leaned over and whispered, "I'll come up with more fun ways for us to say thanks to each other later."

"Cut that out," Daniel growled. "Everything's at stake now, so focus on the job."

Daniel led them into his office and fired up his computer.

"Are we really going to steal this information? The damage that'll do…" she said slowly.

Daniel shook his head. "No, not steal. I didn't want to say this in front of Steve, but we're just going to borrow some screens and fake the information. The trick will be accessing the database and seeing the initial layout so we can make it all look authentic."

After typing in several personal passwords and running an intrusion program, he finally turned around. "I'm no hacker, but I learned a few things from the kid we hired to work here," he said. "I'm now into the DMV's system. That was the easy part. Lori, can you show me which database I need to access?"

Lori took the mouse and led him to the right directory. The massive file contained recorded personal information for every current vehicle owner in the state. She could enter her user name to gain another half step, but to actually open the file and download the data required the right password.

"I'll try to run a password-generating program now," Daniel said. "Maybe I'll get a hit and be able to get a look at the next screen."

"I should warn you that with our system you'll get three tries," Lori said. "After the third wrong attempt, you won't be able to get back into the program using this computer. My user name will be considered compromised, too, which will shut me out, as well."

"So the mass attack won't work," Gene said, "but we can still play a good bluff. The bad guys haven't seen those screens, either, so mimic what you can and fake the rest, generating phony names, social security numbers and addresses. Can you duplicate the initial screens to make them look like the real deal?"

"Sure," Daniel said. "It's part of the training we give our IT people—how to recognize phony but authentic-looking websites used to con people."

Daniel inserted a flash drive and, with a few

clicks of the mouse, captured the images. "Now we'll add names and phony social security numbers."

"I know the layout of the individual records, so that solves our next problem. Do you have a randomizing program?" Lori asked.

"Yeah, plus something even better. What I'll do is insert names from the Albuquerque metro area residential pages of the phone book. Those are public record, so I can download that data easily enough. Then I'll generate and insert fake social security numbers for each address," Daniel said.

Ten minutes later, Daniel removed a new flash drive from the computer, then turned to Lori. "What do you think?"

She took a quick look, checking her own name and address within the fake database. "It sure looks like the real deal, and my social isn't even close. Considering that we have no way of getting into the actual system without locking it up and sending out flags, it's our only shot," she said.

"Okay, let's get going," Daniel said. "We still have a long night ahead."

Once they waved goodbye to the guard and started the return drive to Steve's house, Gene gave Daniel a stony look. "Lori's *not* going to make this transfer."

"That's for me to decide," Lori said softly.

Gene shook his head. "*No.* Risking another person being taken hostage—especially someone like you who's potentially an even more valuable asset to the kidnappers—doesn't make sense. We'd be trading lives, that's all. I've got a much better idea."

Chapter Twenty-Two

Lori handed the flash drive to Steve. "You're all set."

Steve checked his watch. "Daylight's coming soon and we're an hour away from where they want to meet. We have to get going right now."

"Slow down," Paul said. "We have to call the police first and make sure they'll bring us some backup. Hartley P.D. has a team of detectives who've been trying to track down these identity thieves for weeks. Believe me, officers will respond ASAP."

"No way," Steve said. "The kidnappers might spot the cops, and if that happens, Sue will get caught in the cross fire. I'm not putting her at greater risk than she's already in."

Paul shook his head. "The detectives won't do anything stupid, and more importantly, they're trained to deal with situations like these. You guys aren't. We need the officers. Once the suspects have what they want, they might just decide to eliminate all the loose ends."

"Paul's right," Daniel said. "We have to cover every possible angle. Paul, get law enforcement, whether it's FBI, state police or someone else, to provide a couple of snipers."

"Steve, once it starts to go down you're going to have to stall as long as possible," Gene said. "Tell them that you're the one who's going to hand over the flash drive and demand that they bring out Sue." He then looked at Lori. "*You* stay back by the van. Let them see you, but don't come out into the open. Daniel and I will be covering you and Steve, and hopefully we'll have some law enforcement people in position by then, as well."

"I've got two ballistic vests in my office," Daniel said. "Lori, one's for you. Steve, you'll wear the other one."

He shook his head. "No way. If I come out wearing something like that, they'll know something's up."

"It's a lightweight Kevlar vest, the kind that fits under a shirt. It won't show, but it'll still protect you."

"We'll keep you current on our location and plans," Gene told Paul, "but we're counting on you to bring the cavalry."

LORI SAT IN THE PASSENGER seat as Steve drove through the gates at Daniel's place. Gene was in the back, within arm's reach of Steve, but out of sight. The gates were just closing behind them when Steve's phone rang. He answered immediately.

"Put it on speaker," Gene ordered in a whisper-soft tone.

"Change of location," the man at the other end snarled. "Go to the wrecking yard a mile east of the fairgrounds, south side of the road. You've got fifteen minutes."

Steve looked at Gene, who mouthed, *thirty.*

"Huh?" Steve answered.

"Fifteen minutes, or your wife's history."

Finally Steve caught on. "I can't get there in less than thirty minutes. I'm on the west side of town, on my way to the landfill, like you said before."

"You've got twenty-five, and make sure it's just you and the woman. Anything else and it's all over for Sue Farmer."

The next thing they heard was silence.

"We have time," Gene said, checking his watch. "We'll take the truck bypass and can be there in twenty. Now let's get those vests and update Paul. He'll need to reposition our backup in a hurry."

TWENTY-THREE MINUTES LATER, Gene slipped out the back of the slow-moving van, rifle in hand. He quickly ducked between two junked school buses as Steve turned down a long row of squashed, wrecked vehicles stacked three high.

Steve, with Lori beside him, parked, then waited for further instructions.

Gene looked all around him. Paul was out there somewhere among the wreckage, but the police, who couldn't use their emergency lights or sirens without giving themselves away, were still en route. Steve and Lori would need to play for even more time.

Alert for any sign of the kidnappers or their vehicle, Gene slipped between two rows of smashed cars, moving slowly along and keeping one eye on the van.

"Nothing yet," Lori whispered over the handheld radio.

Gene waited, listening for any sign of human activity. There was a slight breeze, and a wind-blown piece of paper flapped atop a wrecked sedan, trapped below a windshield wiper like a neglected moving violation. Somewhere, metal creaked, like an open door swaying back and forth.

He then heard the faint tone of Steve's cell phone, and Lori's whispered, "Speaker."

"We see you. Turn your lights off, then drive slowly to the end of the row. Stop beside the pile with the white pickup on top," the kidnapper ordered.

Everything was quiet again, then Lori whispered, "Get that, guys?"

"Copy," Daniel whispered over his radio.

"Steve, go real slow, then stop a little short of the white pickup. Stay in the van as long as you can," Gene told him over the radio.

Gene looked around, knowing Daniel was somewhere opposite him. His brother had used another road to get to the wrecking yard and had parked outside, intending to scale the fence.

"You getting all this, Paul?" Gene whispered.

"Four," Paul confirmed in law enforcement shorthand for ten-four.

Squeezing between stacks of vehicles and stepping around and between the sharp metal edges of the wrecks made for tough going. More than once Gene had to risk circling around the outside of the row because the stacks were too close to allow for safe passage. At least he was able to stay in shadow.

Finally Gene caught a glimpse of an intact vehicle, a big SUV, parked at the end where the driveway circled the center stacks. Its headlights were out, but the driver's-side window was down and he could see the faint glow of what looked to be a lit cigarette just beyond the steering wheel.

He watched Steve stop the van about fifty feet from the SUV, near what looked like the wrecking yard's tow truck, then turn off the engine.

"Here we go," Lori whispered. "You there, Gene?"

"Just a heartbeat away, Lori," he whispered back. "I have to turn off my radio now or they might hear. Love you."

She drew in a breath. That was the first time he'd actually said it. Unfortunately, the timing really sucked.

"Bring the woman and the flash drive," the male voice from the SUV yelled out the window.

Gene caught movement across the way, to the right of a wrecked semi beside the tow truck. A man was standing in the shadows. Although he didn't know Daniel's or Paul's exact positions, this clearly was neither of them. The guy was too short and stocky, and from what he could see of the weapon, the man had a shotgun, not a rifle.

"Nothing happens until I see my wife," Steve yelled, his voice cracking at the end. "Nothing else matters to me but her. I'll drive away unless I see Sue's okay." To add emphasis to his threat, he switched on the ignition.

"Way to go, Steve," Gene whispered to himself. He had his rifle trained on the man with the shotgun standing in the shadows.

"Turn off your engine," the kidnapper ordered in a booming voice. "I'll bring your wife and you send out the woman with the data. Then we'll make the exchange." There was a brief pause, then he added, "Cross me and you'll all die."

Gene kept his sights on the man with the shotgun as he shifted to one side, angling for a clear shot. To his surprise, Gene saw that the man wasn't wearing a mask.

As the SUV's driver came out, he tossed his cigarette on the ground, then brought out a handgun. With his free hand, he reached back into the SUV and hauled out a stocky blonde with tape over her mouth.

"Here she is, Farmer," the driver yelled, pushing her toward the van. "Your turn. Send the woman."

As Gene drew closer, he saw that the SUV's driver wasn't wearing a mask, either. Sue had seen what both men looked like, and so would Lori and Steve in just a few seconds. The kidnappers' plans were suddenly crystal clear to him. They planned to kill everyone once the exchange was made.

Steve climbed out of the van, according to plan. Then Lori, who was supposed to stay back, stepped out the passenger side.

"No," Gene muttered under his breath. He thumbed the radio, signaling Dan, who was somewhere close by. "They've shown their faces, which means they're going to get bloody."

"I'll create a diversion," Dan whispered, "and you move in. Steve's too pumped to think clearly, but maybe Lori will remember the backup plan."

Gene hooked the radio back to his belt, then inched closer, feeling with his thumb to make sure the safety on his rifle was off. The guy with the shotgun stepped out into full view, right into his sights.

"Here we are," Steve called out, stepping over beside Lori. "And here's the flash drive," he said, holding it up. "Once my wife is next to me, I'll throw you the drive."

"Dumb ass, we're done bargaining." The driver raised the pistol up to Sue's head.

"No!" Lori screamed.

Suddenly the scene was flooded by bright headlights. The tow truck roared to life and swerved toward the man with the shotgun.

"Drop!" Gene yelled.

Steve stood there, confused, but Lori fell like a stone to the ground just as Sue grabbed her captor's gun hand.

Gene raced past Lori, who'd raised her head to look around. "Stay down!" he yelled.

Sue was struggling with the driver, wrestling for the pistol, when Gene arrived. He swung the butt of his rifle, slamming the guy across the face with the wooden stock. The blow carried so much force, the man's feet left the ground.

Daniel leaped from the wrecker, aiming his pistol at the guy he'd knocked down with the tow truck. "Stay away from that shotgun," he yelled.

"Everyone freeze," someone yelled from the passenger side of the SUV.

Gene's smile faded as he realized this was no backup cop. The angry man was a third kidnapper, and the short-barreled carbine he held was aimed right at him. When he stepped out, Gene recognized him instantly.

"Harvey?" Steve said, sounding dazed.

"Yeah, I'm tired of working for peanuts. This is

my go-to-hell money," Harvey yelled. "Hand me that flash drive. Now!"

"Not a chance. Drop your weapon," Paul ordered, coming into view from Harvey's left, the red beam of a laser sight playing over the big man's rib cage.

As Harvey looked down at the beam, Gene redirected his own aim. Now it was a standoff.

"You're outgunned, man. Put it down," Gene growled.

"*Way* outgunned," Sergeant Chavez yelled, coming around the SUV with a riot gun. Beside him was an armed state policeman aiming an assault rifle. "Lower your weapons—slowly."

The other kidnappers, who'd recovered their weapons as soon as Harvey had come out of cover, placed their guns on the ground and were quickly placed under arrest.

"We've been looking for you punks," Chavez said as the criminals were lined up facing the SUV, then handcuffed.

Steve gave his wife a hug, then stepped forward. "Better take me, too. These kidnappers forced me to do some terrible things."

Chavez waved him over. "You and your wife will ride up front with me, Mr. Farmer. No handcuffs are necessary. I'm leaving any charges up to the D.A." He turned to Lori. "We'll need a statement from you, of course."

"I understand, but since Steve was coerced I won't be pressing charges," she said.

Chavez nodded, then motioned for the other officers to take away the prisoners.

Gene reached Lori just then and pulled her into his arms.

"I can deal with a bucking stallion and face down a seven-hundred-pound bear, but woman, you're too much to handle."

"But that won't keep you from trying, will it?"

"What do you think?" Tilting her chin up, he lowered his mouth to hers.

Epilogue

It was midmorning as she followed Gene up a barely discernible trail behind the house at Copper Canyon. They hadn't slept, but she wasn't the least bit tired.

"Each of my brothers had a place in Copper Canyon that was special to him. I'm taking you to mine," he said, then, meeting her gaze, added, "I've never brought anyone else here."

Excitement rippled through her as they entered a tiny gap in the cliff side, not much more than a crack in the massive formation.

"Tell me more about where we're going," she said, trying not to feel claustrophobic in the tall, narrow enclosure. The feeling quickly disappeared as the gap between the walls began to widen and they proceeded into the cavity.

Before long they were walking along a grass-covered path bordered by narrow pines that had managed to survive despite the restricted sunlight. It was cool in this natural courtyard, though there was no sign of a breeze.

"We weren't allowed to mark anything in or

around the house, but I wanted to leave something behind that would show that I'd walked this path, that I'd been here." Gene stopped beside a big hollow in the cliff side carved out by weathering and erosion. In its center was a carefully constructed mound of rocks almost two feet high.

"Cairns of rocks just like this one are all over the Navajo Nation and represent someone's passage. Mine was one of the soul as much as of the body," he said, gazing at it, lost in thought. "After each battle and victory in my life, I added a rock."

"Then this is a place of strength and courage," she said quietly.

"That's exactly what it is," he said. "Our legends tell us that rocks are all that remain of the monsters that once walked the earth and preyed on mankind. Each rock on that cairn represents a ghost, or memory, of my own past that I fought and conquered."

She looked at him, wondering why he'd brought her here at this particular time. There was something else on his mind—she could feel it with each beat of her heart.

"The war I fought, like the one you've struggled with, was mostly inside me." He handed her a small stone. "This is a rock a bear turned over. It's special, and we use them in our War Ceremony. I want you to place it on the top. It'll mark your own victory over the ghosts of *your* past. Let this become a place where our spirits join to celebrate a new beginning."

She took the flat stone from his hands and carefully set it upon the stack of rocks already there. "I've spent my life running away from myself," she said, turning to face him. "I was afraid to love because when I had, all I'd found in return was pain. Then you came into my life and everything changed. I love you, Gene, and for me, there's no turning back."

As Raven cried out overhead, he pulled her into his arms and kissed her in a slow, pervasive way that left her tingling all the way down to her toes.

"Then we'll go forward together. I love you, *sawe*."

With a sigh, Lori melted against him. "The Bear and the Raven. Maybe we'll start a legend of our own."

As the morning breeze blew over Copper Canyon, the shadows faded, and in the distance, Bear woke to Raven's song.

* * * * *

LARGER-PRINT BOOKS!
GET 2 FREE LARGER-PRINT NOVELS PLUS
2 FREE GIFTS!

Harlequin®

INTRIGUE®

BREATHTAKING ROMANTIC SUSPENSE

YES! Please send me 2 FREE LARGER-PRINT Harlequin Intrigue® novels and my 2 FREE gifts (gifts are worth about $10). After receiving them, if I don't wish to receive any more books, I can return the shipping statement marked "cancel." If I don't cancel, I will receive 6 brand-new novels every month and be billed just $5.24 per book in the U.S. or $5.99 per book in Canada. That's a saving of at least 13% off the cover price! It's quite a bargain! Shipping and handling is just 50¢ per book in the U.S. and 75¢ per book in Canada.* I understand that accepting the 2 free books and gifts places me under no obligation to buy anything. I can always return a shipment and cancel at any time. Even if I never buy another book, the two free books and gifts are mine to keep forever.

199/399 HDN FERE

Name _____

(PLEASE PRINT)

Address _____ Apt. #

City _____ State/Prov. _____ Zip/Postal Code

Signature (if under 18, a parent or guardian must sign)

Mail to the **Reader Service:**
IN U.S.A.: P.O. Box 1867, Buffalo, NY 14240-1867
IN CANADA: P.O. Box 609, Fort Erie, Ontario L2A 5X3

Not valid for current subscribers to Harlequin Intrigue Larger-Print books.

**Are you a subscriber to Harlequin Intrigue books
and want to receive the larger-print edition?
Call 1-800-873-8635 today or visit www.ReaderService.com.**

* Terms and prices subject to change without notice. Prices do not include applicable taxes. Sales tax applicable in N.Y. Canadian residents will be charged applicable taxes. Offer not valid in Quebec. This offer is limited to one order per household. All orders subject to credit approval. Credit or debit balances in a customer's account(s) may be offset by any other outstanding balance owed by or to the customer. Please allow 4 to 6 weeks for delivery. Offer available while quantities last.

Your Privacy—The Reader Service is committed to protecting your privacy. Our Privacy Policy is available online at www.ReaderService.com or upon request from the Reader Service.

We make a portion of our mailing list available to reputable third parties that offer products we believe may interest you. If you prefer that we not exchange your name with third parties, or if you wish to clarify or modify your communication preferences, please visit us at www.ReaderService.com/consumerschoice or write to us at Reader Service Preference Service, P.O. Box 9062, Buffalo, NY 14269. Include your complete name and address.

HILP11B

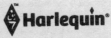